THE GENESIS OF KALKI

Amol Anand Tiwari

Sakāl Publications

THE GENESIS OF KALKI

© Amol Anand Tiwari (2025)

Sakal Media Pvt. Ltd.
595, Budhwar Peth, Pune – 411002, India
www.sakalpublications.com | sakalprakashan@esakal.com

First Edition: January, 2025

This is a work of fiction. Names, characters, places, and incidents are either the product of the author's imagination or are used fictitiously. Any resemblance to actual persons, living or dead, events, or locales is purely coincidental.

The views and opinions expressed in this book are solely those of the author and do not necessarily reflect the views of any organization, publisher, or institution.

ISBN No.: 978-93-48048-34-9

Edited by: Sneha Makharia
Cover Design: Sonu Panda (sonu4565@gmail.com)
Typesetting: MAP Systems, Bengaluru

Printed in India by Sakal Media Pvt. Ltd.

Contents

Author's Note   5

Introduction 7

1. Cause and Effect 11

2. The Story of the Story 23

3. History of the Future 33

4. The Discovery of *Nandak* 43

5. *Karma* 53

6. *Maya* 64

7. *Leela* 75

8. Opium of Success 87

9. *Ekantik* 98

10. Indestructibility 111

11. Full Circle 123

12. Autonomy 134

13. *Abedh* 146

14. The Genesis 156

Epilogue 163

Author's Note

I am writing this note in December of 2024, after completing the book, a few days before it goes to print. I started writing this book in December of 2017, sitting in the balcony of my friend's home in Goa. I used to feel that happy people seldom create art, as they are too busy cherishing the joys of life. To want to create something, you need to have a void or an innate sadness. Unfortunately, or fortunately, I did.

During this duration, this book kept oscillating between crippling self-doubt and reassuring confidence. It got buried many times into the graveyard of promising ideas, but each time got resurrected back with a new life, stronger than before. The final version bears little resemblance to the original idea that I started with, proving to me that a book writes itself and an author is nothing more than a typist taking dictation. This book manifested itself through me.

Why does someone write a book? I have a reasonably successful, comfortable, and fulfilling professional career. Why should I subject myself to intellectual scrutiny? Why should I open an avenue of potential stress? Why undertake a journey that could turn out to be excruciating, arduous and uncertain? These questions echoed in my mind, much like thoughts that crop up during the grueling stretches of a marathon or a challenging trek: Why should one do these things?

Following some personal setbacks, I embarked upon a journey of self-discovery. It was a long, painful, and difficult journey wherein I stripped myself of the multiple fake personalities, I had covered myself under. The outcome was very stark and liberating. Seeing the world—and myself—without any illusion leaves little room for pretension. You lose friends, and you become lonely, but you also become peaceful. You get firmly grounded in truth and become unshakable. I realized this about myself: I am full of ideas, I am good with words, but I am also prone to laziness. I am more of a thinker and maybe a storyteller. And I came to understand that I must write—because I can.

This story is a curated expression of my knowledge, beliefs, ideas, thoughts, and feelings. I come from a legacy of knowledge workers; staying true to that, I have both a responsibility and privilege to express my ideas. As my mind is only a receptor of the idea and not the creator of it, I must express it most earnestly.

Finally, it is the reader that completes the book. So here you are, culminating this journey. In your hands, this book finds its purpose. The ideas presented here now belong to you. And if this book kindles any hope, joy, a warm feeling, an enthusiasm, or a perspective, then my job writing it is fructified. So, thank you for making this book complete. This book is now yours.

Om tat sat.

Introduction

AI is transforming the world at an unprecedented pace. It is no longer a question of if but when AI will assume control of various global processes. What does this mean for humanity? What would a world largely run by AI look like? Would technology help humanity redeem itself, or will it repeat the past evolutionary mistakes?

The world around us is full of violence, inequality, disparity, pain, anguish, and despair. While humanity has accomplished great feats, the summation of our evolutionary journey thus far does not look very good. The times ahead seem bleak, and it is easy to be pessimistic about the future of mankind. Can the rapidly evolving AI technology be a beacon of hope? Can it fix all that's wrong in our world and our civilization once and for all?

In a world dominated by technology and machines, would timeless principles that have been driving humanity for centuries continue to resonate? How will the concepts of family values and human relationships evolve and maintain their relevance in a futuristic world?

This book critically explores these questions through the journey of the protagonist, blending the worlds of advanced AI and the wisdom of Hindu scriptures. By weaving these ideas into a compelling narrative, the book presents some profound spiritual and philosophical concepts in an accessible, contemporary style—offering readers some guidance to navigate through the complexities of our rapidly changing world. Many individuals can strive for self-improvement, ethical decision-making, and conscious living guided by these timeless principles.

It is important that we identify our fears and traumas and heal from them. In the future, self-discovery could become the only definition of success. As the world changes, both at an individual level and at a macro level, we should not only be prepared to embrace the change but ride the wave of this transformation.

This science fiction novel unfolds over fourteen captivating chapters. The story begins in 2034, with the protagonist, an Indian-origin entrepreneur, Pradyumn, unveiling *MayaVerse*, a groundbreaking virtual reality platform. It is powered by *Maya*, a super AI already running the world and would be orchestrating this new virtual reality universe. At this time, Pradyumn is already riding high on the success of the most prominent AI platforms that he has created, *Nandak* and *Karma*, which have already transformed the world.

Chapters two through seven delve into a flashback of the future, tracing events from the present day to 2034. They reveal the evolution of the aforesaid AI platforms while developing Pradyumn's personal journey, which includes his relationships with his parents, wife, daughter, and two colleagues.

Each chapter elucidates, with optimism, how the world slowly becomes a better place, step by step, led by AI technology. An uninfluenced and unbiased AI system running this world is presented as humanity's last harbinger of hope. And AI will indeed transform the world into a truly beautiful place.

From chapter eight onwards, the narrative intertwines advanced technological progress with the enduring power of human emotions and family values. It continues to affirm that technology was never a bad thing, but humans made it bad with their greed and personal agendas. And that human emotions will continue to stay supreme in the technology-led future.

According to Hindu scriptures, *Kalki's* arrival is an inevitable part of the larger cosmological cycle. It will take place to restore righteousness and destroy the wicked, ending the current age of darkness and moral decline. This idea that a divine figure will come to save humanity is a common theme in many religious traditions, offering a vision of hope and redemption for future generations. That good will eventually triumph over evil is a common denominator that gives humanity hope.

The utopic world that AI accomplishes, raises the query of whether Super AI could be *Kalki's* promised avatar. The book throws some subtle yet definite clues. There are also a lot of easter eggs hidden all over for curious readers.

The book is fast-paced and lean, with very few deeply connected characters. The story is kept simple, where sci-fi meets scriptures, philosophy meets fiction, and technology meets spirituality. Your thoughts matter. Please connect and share your ideas and views on tgok.in or use #TheGenesisOfKalki on social media.

You can also scan the QR code at the end of each chapter for a glossary and to interact, collaborate and contribute.

1

Cause and Effect

"OM," the baritone sound was floating over the pin-drop silence of a massive crowd that was waiting with an expectation-filled curiosity.

It is *Basant Panchami* of *Samvat* 2090, two days before the 85th Republic Day of India. *Bharat Mandapam*, the world's grandest convention hall in New Delhi, is filled with a global audience.

Pradyumn Tripathi walks on the stage with a giant LED screen as the backdrop. A round spotlight tracks his medium-built body, and the repeating sound of *OM* on the powerful sound system provides a soothing ambiance.

Pradyumn, or PraT as he is more popularly known, is the CEO of a technology conglomerate, *Aksharmala,* one of the largest companies in the world by its market capitalization. He starts his keynote, with the same famous words of Swami Vivekananda from 1893 when he spoke at the World's Parliament of Religion.

"Sisters and brothers, the theory of evolution should have been a hypothesis. It was a well-believed theory for centuries, but now it has been reduced just to a prolonged manifestation of the human species' arrogance and a false sense of superiority. The survival of the fittest, or the survival of the wicked?

It's like saying that an uneducated homeless mugger who shot an Ivy League MBA Investment banker on the streets of New York, is superior to him. It's like the mugger on the streets, Joe Chill, was superior to Thomas Wayne of Gotham City, just because in the end, Joe survived, and Thomas did not."

The DC Comics reference created murmured laughs from the audience.

"For centuries, it was believed, that plants were the lowest form of existence. If a large part of a tree is amputated, it grows back. A significant feature missing in the subsequent so-called higher forms of life. A tree creates an ecosystem around its being, therefore not needing any movement for itself. Plants create their own food, a significantly more mature form of existence than the nomadic so-called higher forms of life.

Animals also have very well-defined behavior patterns, and simple and accurate forms of communication, and collaboration. Have you ever noticed thousands of ants collaborating to build an ant hill, or bees making a hive? It takes millions of dollars and years of rigid training to get a group of humans in a large corporation to follow such discipline and process adherence.

Humans think they are superior because they have intelligence. Can six humans draw a line each to draw a perfect hexagon, like the bees do in their hive? Can an average human tell by looking at the potato crop without plucking a root, if the potato underneath is ripe? Any average porcupine, in fact, their entire species, can identify a single ripe root in a field full of crops. Is this intelligence insignificant?

I know I am oversimplifying these things. As humans, we have achieved a lot, from fire to the wheel, to medicines, to nuclear energy, to space exploration, to the Internet, and now to Super AI. All this is driven by the quest for knowledge. We think this is what makes us superior to animals and plants.

What if animals already know what we are trying to figure out? What if there is some super cosmic intelligence that these animals and plants already have access to? They don't seem lost like we are. All plants shed their leaves when it's autumn, live in hibernation without leaves or photosynthesis during winter, and bloom during spring. They don't need a notification system reminding them when it's time. Birds fly every year from Siberia to India without any navigation satellites and return after the sojourn."

PraT was an authority in the area of artificial intelligence (AI), as that hubristic term was still in vogue. His algorithms and models not only helped create the most sophisticated Intelligent Systems in the world, but they also made him a centillionaire, an obnoxious title that evolved for people whose wealth was in hundreds of billions of dollars.

Some people are proud intellectuals, while some love public attention. Some are politically active, and some are unapologetically rich. PraT was all of the above. The world was standing at a cusp where machines and Intelligent Systems were almost running the whole world, and he was the biggest proponent of this movement. He believed the world would be a better place if it were run by machines.

PraT had already become a cult figure. His fan following was much larger than any of the sporting legends, film stars, politicians, or artists. The fanatic fan-following was unprecedented and almost of a religious cult kind. He had the power to start a global mass movement and he knew that. There was no household in the modern world that did not have a product from his company. He was a modern-day hero who was about to take his biggest leap.

People today were sure enough to have rejected the flaws of mankind's past mistakes but were unsure about which way to go next. They knew what they didn't believe in anymore, but they also didn't know what to believe in. Like education, once you understand something you can't unlearn it. Like swimming or cycling—you can't pretend to forget it. The keynote was being streamed and viewed by millions across the world. All these people were now empty glasses of faith waiting to be filled with some new nectar that PraT had unknowingly discovered and offered to distribute in a liberal quantity to whoever was seeking it.

The spotlight was on PraT. His straight, spiked-up hair was glowing under the flashy light. His grey eyes peeped out of his very expensive glasses. He had the glow of a teenager, well-hydrated skin, and a neatly shaven, fair, and flawless face. He was wearing his signature white polo t-shirt with his company logo on the left side of his chest, comfortable chino pants, and loafers. He continued,

"All that a dog aspires for is food, sunshine, and space to run around, while not getting annoyed by the gibberish sounds of English coming out of his human's mouth and tolerating stupid names given to it with sagacious humility. Dogs don't even need to have ambition, passion, and a purpose. They just need a belly rub.

Unlike all other animal species, humans unfortunately don't follow the laws of nature. As civilizations evolved, instead of living in harmony with nature, mankind went on a manipulation spree. Agriculture, hunting, sailing, trade, and barter were all governed by the natural cycles. But the madness of creating more than the natural cycles permitted led humans to the illusion of scarcity and malfeasance of greed and exploitation. Then humans, like parasites, began to breed beyond the natural equilibrium and disturbed the natural balance.

A parasite's net worth is dependent on the host it's breeding upon. And humans thought they owned this world."

The audience was listening with rapt attention. He continued his keynote address,

"The worst then came in the form of the Industrial Revolution. Humans invented materials that would not decompose, food that was not naturally grown, and diseases that never existed naturally. This myopic view of existence is very specific to humans who started feasting on their very habitat. Much like viruses and bacteria.

It was during the 19th and 20th centuries when humans screwed up everything.

Every human being is unique and does not necessarily conform to any specific behavior pattern. Unlike other species, we need very specific laws to align ourselves and create a synergy where we can coexist and collaborate. To bring this symmetry, we have always needed models such as religion, societal norms, legal systems, and corporate regulations to govern us. Once a group of humans is bound by these rules, they work very well and have the potential to achieve great feats. These groups of symmetrical people then thrive and grow.

Then, there are a few who amass power out of these multitudes of human potential and preside over these models. They then start to manipulate these delicately balanced systems to create asymmetry to benefit themselves, eventually creating a disbalance, leading to the self-destruction of the whole construct itself.

Labor needs capital to be productive, and capital requires labor to grow. Yet this symbiotic relationship transmuted into a battle of absolutism and resulted in the Left vs the Right.

The anti-monarchy revolutionist Napoleon Bonaparte became an Emperor himself. The religion of the Desert Fathers, who sought truth through ardor and penance by renouncing all luxury and vanity, ended up creating magnificent cathedrals and immense wealth for the church. Islam proclaimed the equality of all mankind but has seen perhaps the fiercest inter-sectorial rivalries amongst its followers. Buddha cautioned his followers not to make him a God, and that is what they precisely did.

Many civilizations flourished for a while and then destroyed themselves. All well-intended efforts for equality created only disparity. This prolonged disparity sparked revolutions, resulting in the collapse of civilizations, obsolescence of religions and centuries of conflict among people, fiefdoms, kingdoms, and nations. Most wars were not fought for resources but around ideological supremacy and related fallacies.

As a species, all humans are the same, and yet, every human being is different.

Everyone is different, but also equal.

There is symmetry and asymmetry.

The two opposite poles united in an endless loop. Like a snake eating its own tail.

If human history has one consistent trend, it is that humans will never treat each other equally. They are divisive inherently. This is why all models that existed in the history of humans ended up in conflict. The concepts of religion, society, countries, and race are all flawed as none treat everyone as equals. There are always some superior to the rest.

We humans are so plagued with prejudice that we don't find a moth's metamorphosis as spectacular as a butterfly's even though it's the same biological process.

This inherent flaw needs to be fixed in order to reach a sustainable, if not perfect, model for human existence and prevent our decay and apocalypse. We need a new set of rules for humanity, but this time without the flaws. These rules need to be agnostic and fair, where all human beings are equal. We need the dawn of a new world where everyone is equal, across borders, religions, gender, color, or creed.

And technology has the answer. To create a system where all of mankind is objectively equal, we had to take the humans out of the driver's seat."

PraT paused to take a sip of water, which was placed on a highchair in the middle of the stage. He turned back towards the audience and continued,

"As the 21st century arrived, for the first time, technology leveled up the world. Internet, mobile phones, AI, and quantum computing not only changed the world but created one new opportunity to redefine humanity. As technology became more mainstream and autonomous, we could fix a lot of irregularities and malfeasance that plagued humanity, but conflicts continued to persist.

As technology becomes mature enough to run the world without human intervention, would we create another civilizational blunder, or would we finally fix the world?

When we launched the *Karma* platform in 2030, nobody believed that we could create a social network at a world scale and keep it unpolluted with zero human intervention in its operations. It was the first real-time AI algorithm that monitored all users, allowing them to monetize their good and virtuous deeds.

The *Karma* Platform has allowed your actions alone to define you. Your actions alone became your identity and defined your social equity. Everyone was equal and unique at the same time. This platform freed you from all the legacy burden of your bank account, your birth, your color, your gender, your faith, your physical appearance, and your family. You were all what you make of yourself.

As an edge-defining AI system, it kept learning and correcting itself of any flaws, and over the last four years, the *Karma* platform now knows more about human behavior than all of humanity's collective knowledge of many centuries. It has generated deep models by studying the 3 billion users that use it daily. These models have been self-learning with zero human intervention and hence have stayed unbiased, agnostic, and fair.

The success of the *Karma* platform has become the dawn of a new world order where, for the first time in human history, everyone is equal. And technology has been ensuring that."

The audience responded with applause. PraT was speaking the truth that was widely realized and its power could be seen in the satisfaction of 3 billion daily active users of the system. Almost everyone in the audience had transformed their lives for good using his technology and earned significant money in the process.

"Let me share a secret. *Karma* has been the most successful Intelligent System in the world. The essence of the algorithm that runs it is the simple model of Cause and Effect. Everything that happens around us, has a cause and an effect. Every action, or *karma*, has a cause and effect.

The cause for an action has a weighted cost, and so does its effect. Human mind evaluates this cost on a value scale and decides whether to act or not. The effect of each action then becomes the cause for another. The effects of essentially all actions are causes of your next, hence having a compounding effect in your chain of *Karma*.

There are perpetual cascades of causes and effects, and as the pace increases, it becomes difficult to differentiate between what is cause and what is effect. And the value scale of all actions are not commandments that Moses received inscribed in stone by fire, but continuously calibrated by the collated wisdom of humanity.

In essence, every action can have a score associated with it—maybe a positive or a negative score, and every person can accumulate these scores, resulting in a net value that reflects their overall actions at any given point in time.

Similarly, another person's chain of actions comes with their *Karma* score. When we interact with other humans, we add another dimension of complexity to our *Karma* score. These interactions are sometimes direct, and sometimes invisibly indirect. You work with a colleague, which is a direct interaction. But a consumer of your work can be a faceless, nameless individual in some other geography or chronology, which constitutes an indirect interaction. But your *Karma* does interact.

Now blow these out to many billions of humans. The problem then becomes seemingly complex but can still be defined as relationships using graphs and numbers. This web of life is a meandering interaction of *Karma*—each independent yet connected. This world, if you notice is just a very large, connected graph of human interactions. The effects of some actions are immediate and for some, indefinite.

Over the years, our algorithms have perfected these calculations and devised a reliable and fair model to understand human interactions. All weightages to *Karma* are assigned by a self-learning AI engine and it keeps evolving. These calculations are immutable, the scores are all sacrosanct and nothing in the system can be modified. The system cannot be altered to increase the weighted score of any cause or effect. The only way a person can improve the *Karma* score is by improving the actions even though the causes have been unfavorable. This has been the fairest model for human evaluation, ever created. It's just beautiful mathematics, impeccable and pristine.

Over the years, the *Karma* platform has enabled over a billion users to perform good actions and monetize their *Karma* score to pay off their debts, buy new assets, make homes for themselves, and accomplish financial salvation.

And today, on the auspicious day of worship of the Goddess of Knowledge, we extend the *Karma* Platform into the *MayaVerse*. All your interactions inside *MayaVerse* will also affect the ledger of your *Karma* score. Our aim is to allow the goodness of your avatar to be monetized in the metaverse as well.

This is the biggest technological leap that *Aksharmala* has ever taken. We are lifting humanity to a higher orbit today. This is where all our decades of innovations come together. The *Karma* platform, the *Maya* AI, the *MayaVerse*, and our *Maya* Pod will come together and gamify life for you.

We call this update *Leela*. This is something I am super proud of. The *Maya* algorithm will present you with a daily challenge, a simulation of a situation in the *MayaVerse*. And you will have to make some choices and deal with that situation. If your choices are the right ones, you will be able to add to your *Karma* score. If you make sub-optimal choices, your *Karma* score will reduce. Your simulations in the *MayaVerse* will be governed by your *Karma* score. You can be part of some luxurious simulations or real hardship simulations, all depending upon the sequence of choices you make. You can always elevate yourself in the *MayaVerse* simply by beginning to make the right choices. It's all mathematics of causes and effects.

Yes, we are simulating life for you and this time it will be absolutely fair."

This moment was nothing short of Steve Jobs launching the Mac at the Flint Center in Cupertino, on January 24, 1984, and it was no coincidence that Pradyumn chose the same day, 50 years later, to launch something he believed was his biggest endeavor yet. He almost emulated Steve Jobs from the iPhone launch and wanted to perform similar theatrics, and he was acutely successful.

A pandemonium erupted of the kind that was seen in the old world of horse races or boxing matches. With hands spread out fully, face tilted upwards, PraT was indeed feeling like God incarnate. Amidst a roaring applause, he started walking away from the stage, saying, "Let's make this world beautiful again. Let all of humanity live like a happy family. *Vasudhaiva Kutumabkam*" and disappeared backstage.

The silence of his empty home was broken by a screeching hydraulic sound from the opening of the casket like Pod, out of which emerged Pradyumn—dressed in his ill-fitting Batman boxer shorts and a white thread across his shoulder, his *Janeu*. He had brown eyes, a receding hairline, an awkward balding patch, and an unkempt salt-and-pepper beard, which was more salt than pepper. With abundant body hair and a generous waistline bulging with abdominal fat, he totally conformed to the stereotypical image of a middle-aged Indian software professional.

He steps out of the *Maya* Pod and walks into the kitchen. He pours himself a coffee and walks to his balcony, cherishing the view of the Kinnaur range from his small home in the Himalayan city of Kalpa, in Himachal Pradesh, India.

This was the real world, where PraT was Pradyumn Tripathi. There was nobody in Bharat Mandapam's auditorium. Everyone watched the keynote from their homes, being broadcast in the *MayaVerse*. Pradyumn delivered the keynote from his home, lying in his *Maya* Pod.

The applause was real. It was just not in the auditorium in New Delhi. But he heard it in his very body of nerves and muscles.

Pradyumn had a smirk on his face as he reflected on his performance with nervous confidence. Whatever the future had in store for him, he seemed ready for it.

2

The Story of the Story

Chandauli town is about 30 kilometers southeast of Varanasi. Varanasi, or Banaras as it's popularly called, is the oldest living city on earth. In ancient times, this blessed area south of the divine river Ganga was known as Magadha and was the epicenter of knowledge and wisdom.

Vyas Mani Tripathi, a mathematics teacher in the local school, and his wife Sarada Devi, daughter of a Sanskrit Pandit and his homemaker wife, were blessed with their first child – a boy - after five years of their marriage.

Vyas Mani had lost his parents when he was a child. He had no uncles and siblings and was anxious to have a son so that his lineage could survive. As happens at the time of birth in any Brahmin family, or for that matter, in most Hindu families, a horoscope was charted to record the celestial placements at the time of birth. The priest said the name starting from the letter pa would be auspicious. Vyas Mani asked his wife, who was more knowledgeable in such matters, to name their son.

Sarada had heard her father chanting the prayer songs of Lord Vishnu and was familiar with the names Vasudev, Sankarshan,

Pradyumn, and Aniruddh from those songs. When she asked her father to explain these four names, he said, "Vasudev is a four-armed form of incorporeal God. Sankarshan is God's brother, a human form – not a God himself but God-like. Pradyumn is the mortal son of God, and Aniruddh is the progeny. Reserving Aniruddh for her future grandson's name, Sarada Devi named her child Pradyumn. The couple had no other child after him.

Pradyumn grew up in Chandauli, studying in the school where his father was employed. He loved learning Sanskrit from his mother at home. He was a healthy and active child and good at his studies. No concepts posed a challenge to him throughout his academic years. He was comfortable in all his academic subjects as though a scholar revising his own thesis. He was not great at sports, and laziness was the primary reason for that. He was well-natured, and he was widely loved by everyone as a child. He was amicable, quiet, wiser than all children, disciplined, and thirsty for knowledge. He spent most of his growing years learning scriptures outside of the curriculum. Vedic mathematics and its techniques particularly excited him, probably because of his father's influence and sublime teaching.

He cracked the JEE Advanced exam like a walk in the park, with a good rank, and got into the most coveted Computer Science Engineering program at the Indian Institute of Technology (IIT), Kanpur. His reason for choosing the college was its proximity to Chandauli, which would allow him to visit his parents every month without traveling much.

That he obviously never did. He excelled at his studies and expectedly became an ace programmer in his college. He built programs and tools for all the problems he saw around him and became a student leader because of his extraordinary skills without fighting any student body elections. He was widely regarded as a genius, and many of his friends and classmates, even professors, knew secretly that he would one day make a name for himself.

After graduation, out of reverence for his father, Pradyumn chose Advanced Mathematics for the Integrated Master's and Ph.D. program in the Department of Mathematics at the Indian Institute of Science (IISc) in Bangalore. His parents came to see him off at the Mirzapur railway station when he boarded his train to Bangalore.

At IISc, Pradyumn fell in love with a Kannadiga girl, Prabhavati, who was also doing her Master's in mathematics there. His parents readily consented to their marriage, though Sarada Devi was a little hesitant about the dietary habits of the Kannadigas. But after ascertaining that Prabhavati came from a family of devout vegetarians, she acquiesced.

Pradyumn focused on machine learning and intelligent systems as his area of research and soon became a well-known name in the subject. His research papers were widely cited and eventually picked up by frontline R&D companies for their product development. He soon got identified by Mutex Corporation, who gave him a pre-placement offer he could not refuse. Soon, Pradyumn and Prabhavati moved to Fremont, California.

A year later, in 2010, the couple was blessed with a girl child. A little disappointed for being unable to use Aniruddh, the name she reserved for her grandchild, Sarada named her beloved granddaughter Rhea after Goddess Lakshmi, the goddess of wealth, prosperity, and abundance. And the family was indeed blessed with all of that and more.

Pradyumn invited his parents, Vyas Mani and Sarada, to live with them for some time. It was their first time traveling outside of India, and they opted to visit from September to November so that they could celebrate all major festivals together. Sarada even packed puja material in her luggage. Pradyumn booked a business class round-the-world ticket to bring them from New Delhi to San Francisco via London and fly them out over the Pacific via Singapore.

Pradyumn, Prabhavati, and Rhea came to the SFO airport to receive them. Growing up as an active and well-mannered girl, Rhea developed an instant bond with her grandmother. Vyas liked the weather—it was sunny, the sky was clear of clouds, and the air smelled healthy. After spending a week mostly at home, it was time to look around. San Francisco was fast-paced. Vyas and Sarada found the speed of life in San Francisco rather intimidating.

Vyas and Sarada laughed their heart out when Pradyumna took them to Crooked Street with eight hairpin turns, and Vyas felt spellbound looking at the Golden Gate Bridge. He could only say, "O my God, it is even bigger than our Howrah Bridge."

But the best interaction happened when Pradyumn showed his father the Mutex Glass. Pradyumn was the manager of the product development team. They were trying to create an eyewear that had a camera mounted on it. Whatever a user would see through the Glass, would also be seen by the onboard camera. The information would be extracted from those images in real-time. So, if a user sees a person in front of him, the Glass lens would also show additional details about that person, like his name, age and social profile. If the user was driving, the Glass would overlay the map on the lens, so that the user could follow the right directions.

Pradyumn arranged a small demo for Vyas at his office. Tenzin Dorji, a Tibetan who grew up in the US and was also another project manager of the Glass project, mounted the Glass and demonstrated how to carry out operations that were previously done by smartphones, such as making video calls, scheduling meetings, taking pictures, checking the weather, and getting directions. The glass used voice commands or other gestures to get user inputs, and the information was projected onto the Glass lens right in front of the user's field of vision. Vyas tried it himself, and found it fascinating and distasteful at the same time.

Tenzin was the hardware lead on the Mutex Glass project, while Pradyumn led the software team. Both great minds got together to build what they saw as a world-altering moon-shot project. Pradyumn was creating the drivers for the projection technology and the software that would process the images being captured from the onboard camera and extract information and intelligence from those images.

The father-son duo had a sumptuous lunch at the cafeteria. However, Vyas left the campus rather withdrawn.

Pradyumn was surprised to see his father go into a reflective mood after using the Glass. Then he said as if murmuring, "*Yeh to Maya bhedi hai* (this will break all illusions)." Vyas Mani found the Glass revolting rather than appealing because persons using such eyewear may secretly record and broadcast private conversations, use facial recognition to identify strangers in public and get their information before interacting with them.

That night, father and son sat under the clear and starry California sky. Eager to talk to his father, Pradyumn asked Vyas Mani Tripathi why he called the MutexGlass as *Maya bhedi*?

What is wrong if we break the *Maya Jaal* (illusionary web around us) and see the truth as is?

His mother was also aptly listening while Prabhavati was playing with Rhea inside.

Vyas Mani, taking on the role of a teacher, gave a lengthy answer. "*Maya* is the illusion that shapes this universe and how life works. The reality is indeed unpalatable and difficult to accept. For example, every child who is born will eventually die, but the mother nursing the child with love must be blind to that reality. So, God created *Maya* and made it *abhed* (impenetrable) so that it is no more an option but inevitable, and you are made to see the world in a way that does not scare you, and life goes on, akin to surgery under anesthesia.

The Glass you have shown me is deciphering the information masked behind appearances. Everyone has a right to create an appearance, and you are taking that right away from them. This is a violation of the natural order; it is like robbing, and I don't approve of it."

Pradyumn is offended. How could his father, a teacher in a rundown school in a terribly small town of India, belittle a cutting-edge technology developed in Silicon Valley by the best of the brains on earth, backed by millions of dollars in investment? Conditioned to be obedient and respectful to his father, he, however, curbed his irritation and made a decent argument, "But bold we must be. Hiding facts is not the approach to finding a solution. As we all know, a hare being hunted by dogs puts its head down and considers itself safe. What use is this fake optimism? Living like the hare? Is this the remedy? Closing our eyes doesn't make it dark."

Vyas is in no mood to give up either. "You may say so as you now possess many of life's comforts. In this wonderful world of amenities and splendor, it is very difficult to become a pessimist. Here, I find everyone telling me how wonderful life is– 'Good morning, good evening, have a great day, and so on'– all so cheerful.

Animals feed on plants, humans on animals, and, saddest of all, the powerful people feed on the weak people in the world. This happens everywhere and will continue to happen. And this is *Maya*. By penetrating it, what solution do you find? Looking at a lady through this glass, do you want to know her age? Her history? How disgraceful is this entire enterprise? Truth is not always beautiful."

Pradyumn is pushed to his edge. He is getting angry at his father's cynicism. He must attack now, "Does not *Gita* admit that this world is a mixture of good and evil, happiness and misery, and must we not do whatever we can to increase the good and reduce the bad? And do we do that by living in *Maya*, blind to reality, happy with a veil covering it? What we cannot accept, we cannot fix."

Vyas is surprised at his son's daring stubbornness. It has been a long time since father and son sat together and conversed as they do now. Their belief system is no longer what it was. The fault lines are apparent and deep. But Vyas is in no mood to meekly listen to his successful and rich son.

"What is this disgracefully bad way of doing good? Violating the privacy of people? Throwing away their meticulously constructed masks? Everything around us is a package deal – life and death; pleasure and pain; light and shadow; health and illness, all go together. There will never be a perfectly good or bad world because the very idea is a contradiction. Good and bad are not two cut-and-dried, separate existences. There is not one thing in this world of ours that you can label as good and good alone, and there is not one thing in the universe that you can label as bad and bad alone. The very same phenomenon, which appears to be good now, may appear bad tomorrow. The same thing that causes unhappiness in one person may cause enjoyment in another. The fire that cooks a good meal for a starving man may also burn the hand of the cook or the entire kitchen.

There is nothing absolute in this world, and that's how *Maya* operates. You cannot comprehend the whole of it, and nothing gives you the right to alter what you don't understand fully."

Pradyumn has no answers, but he is seething at the intellectual arrogance of his father. He looked at his mother, who picked up the impasse between father and son and got up, signaling that the discussion was over. They ate their dinner quietly and retired to sleep.

The next day, the work schedule overtook Pradyumn. He had a quick breakfast and left home by seven in the morning. Prabhavati had to attend a parent-teacher meeting at Rhea's school, and the old Tripathi couple soon found themselves staring at each other with blank minds. This time, Sarada started a conversation,

"We keep changing as we grow in life, both outward and inwardly. When we look back at our old selves, we sometimes find those versions of ourselves amusing. What we feel are our defining attributes, our likes and dislikes, which we struggle to hold on to as our unique habits and preferences today may become an embarrassing memory tomorrow. What we vehemently protect today as something close to our hearts may become insignificant tomorrow. What is a work of art today, may appear amateur tomorrow when we are wiser or more proficient. What will define us then?

We are in a condition of hopeless contradiction. What is the point of doing good work? What is good today may turn bad tomorrow in our own eyes. If it is true that you cannot do good without engaging in bad and that every time you attempt to create happiness, you will also create sadness.

We should be proud that Pradyumn is trying to change the world. He is trying to contribute towards a better world, and maybe his optimism is misplaced, and maybe he will fail. However, you should not prophesize that to him. If this is how *Maya* operates, you do your part and learn to be quiet; if not encouraging, play along with the illusion."

Vyas always respected Sarada. Born into a lineage of Vedic scholars, her conversations have always been well-reasoned, like plants rooted in soil. He heard her in rapt attention and conceded to her wisdom and high intellectual level. Indian wives have always had a magical way to fix their arrogant husbands, he wondered.

The sunny day progressed in a good mood. Prabhavati and Rhea were back, and after some rest, the four decided to go out for a drive. They went to Golden Gate National Recreation Area, and after parking the car, they took a ferry to Alcatraz Island. It is indeed an infamous jail where dreaded criminals were imprisoned in the past. They walked about half a kilometer to the Cell House located at the top of the island.

Vyas was feeling a bit tired, so he sat down, looking at the water. It was a wonderful sight. But his mind took him back to the conversation last night with his son and in the morning with his wife. Human existence is indeed a paradox – where there is life, there is death. Here also, there was this jail amid this vast open space. An inmate in this prison, branded a criminal, may well be a thinker with an open and free mind. In fact, most of us are jailed in our minds, though we are living in an illusion of a free world. A lot of human activity only compounds this travesty and does not lessen it.

After another week of happy moments together, Vyas and Sarada returned to India.

Pradyumn suggested to Prabhavati that she must also invite her parents to visit them. She did not answer immediately and, after some reflective moments, expressed that her mother's Parkinson's disease was progressing rapidly, and it was unlikely that they could travel. Pradyumn felt sad and kept quiet.

A few months later, Mutex scrapped the Glass project, puncturing the arrogance of Pradyumn, who saw years of his hard work go completely to waste. This was the first time he had faced failure in his life, and that too for no fault of his. He informed his father of the events over a video call, expecting an I-told-you-so kind of response, but to his surprise, Vyas was mellow and said, "Hard work never goes to waste. Just because the world is not ready for your idea doesn't mean it is a bad one. It's just that the time is not right, and soon it will be. You keep working hard with unflinching focus."

Everyone has different ways to process failure. Tenzin and Pradyumn processed it very differently. Tenzin resigned and took a long break. Pradyumn continued at Mutex but started spending his time on more theoretical research rather than product development.

They would soon realize why failure is important.

Their time will come.

Antah Asti Prarambh. Every end is also the beginning.

3

History of the Future

Vyas was sitting in the lobby of All India Institute of Medical Sciences (AIIMS) in Banaras, attending to Sarada, who was admitted there due to a fracture caused by a fall induced by hypoglycemia. Like most patient attendees, he had plenty of time to pass. Most news channels on the TV in the hospital lobby were cacophonously playing the interview of the 4 astronauts who had just returned from the successful *Gaganyaan* Mission. The same news had been playing in a loop for a few days across all channels with hideous special effects, dramatic background music and loud news anchors. He decided to utilize his time by watching the TED talk Pradyumn had delivered about a month ago, in March 2026. He watched it with pride.

"Humans have always needed a paradigm to group themselves and yet find reasons to divide. These paradigms have historically been driven by meaningless attributes such as language, the color of the skin, region of origin, profession, choice of food, et all. Some paradigms were more significant, albeit equally meaningless, such as gender, country, and religion. All these factors dynamically gain and lose importance circumstantially.

Human civilizations across the world were stories of existence to start with. Myths collated people like thick rainy clouds that dispersed over time like clouds always do. Some civilizations transcended myths and explored reality. Some overcame the existential challenges and pursued excellence. Some expanded their reach through migration and invasion. Some, however, imploded and collapsed. If there was any constant in human history, it was change, and change has accelerated chronologically.

When these isolated civilizations started interacting, the human boundaries of existence expanded. With faster means of long-distance transportation, people started moving across civilizations. These migrations brought civilizations closer to each other. With centuries of these human interactions, humans learned a lot about each other. Many paradigms of human interactions became obsolete, and some new ones took form.

With the Internet, the world did become a flat, level playing field for all people. It created a world where, more than human migration, the human output needed to move around. Civilizational excellence, for the first time, was truly being leveraged. Human skills outreached national borders. For the first time, all humans were close to a shot at equality. The Internet became such a powerful medium to connect human beings that all other paradigms to divide them started to wither.

On the Internet, it didn't matter which country, gender, religion, or race you belonged to. Everyone was equal. The Internet, from being a reflection of your physical reality, soon became a parallel reality. It became a place where you could be truly free. The digital world inside the Internet became the Promised Land.

Almost every human had internet access. And Internet had access to almost every human.

People started living on the Internet. For entertainment, business, learning, social interactions, transactions, and almost everything, they went online. The more people used the Internet, the more the Internet knew about them. From consumers of the service, these users became the service. They became data generators for these Internet companies, which started studying human behavior. The premise was to provide the best Internet experience, but the amount of information they collected about a user could be used for much more. Internet companies soon knew more about you than your best friend. They had more data about you than your government. They had more influence on you than your religion. And the Internet controlled people subconsciously, like the most potent addiction would, through intoxication.

Internet users carried more computation power in their hands than NASA needed to fly the first moon mission. They knew exactly what you were talking about when you typed something on your phone.

The next frontier in technology was for machines to understand spoken words. By listening to millions of users, the natural language processing algorithms became so advanced that any statement spoken by you could be converted to text and understood by a software. What used to be an analog voice signal in traditional phones became digital signals when users started using voice-over Internet services for cheaper communication. When mobile phone apps allowed users to make free phone calls, the conversations became encrypted but also prone to machine learning. The machines started learning from those millions of digital conversations. Soon, the words being understood by machines became sentences, and whole conversations could be summarized by software.

Along with all the other details about the user, such as their exact location, voice modulation, tone, heart rate, and other vitals collected through wearable devices such as digital watches, the algorithms could also decipher whether what was being spoken was true or not.

Home automation assistants made their way into many homes and were listening to every word spoken. All this was done under the veil of anonymity and providing intelligent solutions to mundane tasks. People were happy with the marvel of technology that the Internet of Things (IoT) was, and governments looked the other way by not regulating any of this.

When the Pandemic hit, and the world's interactions started taking place on the Internet, the amount of intelligence that could be gathered was unprecedented. Machines could now very well understand human conversations.

This also led to a decline in physical human interactions as people became more comfortable interacting digitally. This was an anti-pattern. People started moving out of cramped, polluted crippled cities and, in reverse urbanization, moved to rural areas with clean air and open spaces. These folks created autonomous spaces with off-grid clean energy, high-speed satellite-based Internet, and state-of-the-art home automation. Presiding over ill-gotten hoarded wealth, the real estate industry in urban areas finally imploded.

The Internet was the only gateway for these people to the world. That was the only way they had all their social interactions.

It didn't matter how they lived physically anymore. When the Internet knows everything about your life, why can't we structure and leverage this knowledge constructively?

This world is a massive network of human nodes and a web of human interactions. Every event at a node has a ripple effect on the connected nodes of the network. The intensity of this ripple effect varies, but like water in a river, every ripple is also part of an ongoing flow. Humans have a very small view of their interactions with other human beings. Nobody has a full view of this web of life, but the Internet does.

Only the Internet had visibility of billions of humans and their interactions with each other, direct or indirect. Like the *Indrajaal*, the Internet knew more than all humans combined.

Human interactions are very diverse. You have your immediate family and friends who you are directly connected to. You seem to have reasonable intelligence about those folks, so it's easier for you to interact with them.

Then there are people with whom you interact directly but only because you are connected with them via some transaction. Then there are indirect interactions with people whom you don't even know exist but have a complex indirect connection with them, separated by many degrees of separation.

When you book a cab, you will connect with another human but are barely aware of your driver's situation. What is the driver going through right now? How does he feel? Is he alright? Are you safe in his presence? You run into a person inside your apartment's elevator, and you don't know his name or floor. Is he an introvert? Is he having a nice day? Should you tell a joke to cheer him up? The janitor of your child's school gives out that unsafe vibe. What videos does he watch at his house? You have a new colleague at work. If you start a friendship, what is the likelihood he will borrow money from you? The driver of the car right in front of you; did he have a good night's sleep? Is he feeling drowsy from some medication?

The stock you want to buy. Did the manufacturing plant of this company pay lower electricity bills the last few months? Did its employees spend more time at home this quarter?

The Internet had all these intelligences, but it was scattered and unstructured.

With state-of-the-art artificial intelligence, all this information can be structured anonymously, and immense value can be generated. The fear of losing privacy will easily outweigh the benefits of such intelligence. It could make life around us convenient, safe, and more predictable."

Vyas paused the video of the talk when Pradyumn himself emerged in the hospital lobby, rushing in to see his mother. He had just arrived from the airport and was trying to locate his mother's room. Vyas waves at him and comforts him when they meet. He blesses Pradyumn when he touches his feet, even in those tense and anxious moments.

Pradyumn meets Sarada and is relieved to see she is fine and healing fast. But seeing his parents aging rapidly concerns him. He knew it was going to be unthinkable to expect them to move with him to the US. The thought of moving back to India to be closer to them no longer seems that radical.

After the usual time-bound meals in the hospital, the three of them sat together. Amidst the usual small talk, Vyas complemented Pradyumn for the TED Talk and confessed that he agreed with his vision of using technology to make this world a better place. He could now look beyond the obvious skepticism, and once that barrier was crossed, an entire horizon of new ideas opened up, which could lead the transformation of the world.

"How is work? What is it that you are building these days?" asked Vyas.

Pradyumn regularly shared his ideas earnestly in Mutex meetings but somehow failed to create any traction. He was seen as an Indian spiritualist pushing some Vedic ideas into the hardcore technology business. He took all this snubbing in good humor, but he was becoming increasingly impatient.

"Work is great. I am spending most of my time researching and evangelizing new ideas and concepts. I am not building any product or software anymore. Most of my work is theoretical currently," responded Pradyumn.

"Engineers give Demos. Presentations are for MBAs," joked Vyas.

Sarada was amused being the silent onlooker of the friendly father-son banter.

"It always starts with an idea. The idea has come and must, therefore, be acted upon. But it needs funds, enormous funds indeed, and dedicated teams of smart people who believe in this idea. This idea can only work if it's rolled out on a global scale. If this world must become a better place, the transformation should be a very natural celebratory process. And that takes time, and to sustain an idea for a long enough time, we need prolonged and passionate investments, if any AI system, like the Internet, is to become a part of everyone's life."

Ignoring the mechanics and technicality of what Pradyumn was saying, Vyas responded, "If it's God's will, all resources will appear, and all synergies will emerge."

"When?" quipped Pradyumn impatiently.

"That's also God's will. But like Arjuna in exile didn't lose touch with his archery skills; you, too, must keep the edge of your sword shining. Be patient, but be prepared."

Pradyumn was surprised at the support he was receiving from his father. He had grown fearful, perhaps. It is an essential duty of every family to support and nurture their members so that they can outgrow their fears and self-doubt.

"Let me tell you the story of Sampati," interjected Sarada.

"Sampati and Jatayu were divine eagles, nephews of Garuda, and one day, in order to test their powers, they competed to fly towards the Sun. Jatayu was the younger one and flew faster ahead to win the competition, but Sampati realized they would get scorched if they continued to fly toward the Sun. He spread his wings to cover and save Jatayu and, consequently, got burnt. With burnt wings, Sampati fell onto the ground, miserable and immobile.

He was later healed by a sage whom Sampati prayed to for guidance on his path to redemption. Of what use is the life of a magnificent bird that cannot even fly?

The Sage asked Sampati to wait patiently as the purpose of life is decided by the giver of the life. He also asked Sampati to help some monkeys who would approach him for doing God's work. Which monkeys? When? Asked Sampati, but the Sage said nothing. However, with complete faith, Sampati believed the sage and waited.

Sampati kept meditating for 8 millennia inside a cave. One day, he heard Sita crying out Lord Rama's name in distress, abducted by Ravana while flying above him. Helpless due to his disability, he could not rescue Sita.

But when Hanuman and the monkey army came looking for Sita, he knew his moment had arrived. The search party expressed their mission, and just as Sampati narrated the events, his wings reappeared, and he could fly again. He flew with all his might over Lanka and found the exact location of Sita in the Ashok Vatika. Sampati had finally got his redemption."

Most Indian mothers have this innate quality to cherry-pick seemingly simple, almost comical stories from the scriptures and narrate them in simple words as if putting a child to sleep. However, the profound wisdom these stories carry and the accuracy with which these address the concerns in the listener's mind is never accidental.

Sarada continued, relating the story to Pradyumn's query, "You be patient. Some monkeys will come looking for help; they will be God-sent, so help them, and your wings will also grow again. You will receive whatever you need.

God tests the power of your conviction and the sincerity of your ideas by making you feel stuck and helpless. You should continue meditating on your idea and perfecting it. When the time comes, you should be prepared to succeed in a single shot."

Pradyumn felt relieved. Some words act like the pre-dawn light, dispelling the darkness of doubts.

In a few days, the father-son duo got Sarada discharged from the hospital and returned home. Pradyumn made a failed attempt to take his parents to San Francisco for a few days to help with their recovery. As arrogant, confident, and self-reliant parents would, Vyas and Sarada declined.

Pradyumn appointed some support staff and furnished the house with some convenient furniture and appliances. He also installed some home automation gadgets to monitor his parents remotely, with their consent, of course.

It was time for Pradyumn to return. He was charged with new vigor and dropped his fears, insecurities, and impatience. He was peaceful and cheerful. On his return flight, he made himself comfortable in the business class seat and looked out the window. The plane took off eastward and, after gaining a certain altitude, made a U-turn. Pradyumn got a bird's eye view of the divine city of Banaras.

He caught a glimpse of the Majestic Vishwanath Mandir, shining in full glory, now free of all encroachments. The divine Ganga, clean and full, flows north-eastward along its meandering path.

Pradyumn would now be waiting for the monkeys to come.

4

The Discovery of Nandak

Pradyumn suggested that his wife visit her parents during Rhea's annual summer vacation, and Prabhavati gladly accepted the offer. Pradyumn could not get a long break from work, so he would stay back. It was during this period that he decided to spend a weekend amid nature. Just beyond San Francisco is a protected pocket of ancient redwoods on Mt. Tamalpais. It was still cold for him, though, whatever apology of a summer it was in the Bay Area.

Pradyumn checked into a boutique hotel in Marin County on Friday night and pedaled six miles to Muir Woods the next morning. After reaching Bohemian Grove, Pradyumn kept the bicycle on the side and walked past the trail of 250-foot-tall trees up to Mount Tamalpais East Peak.

He lost track of time in the enchanting natural world, but his hunger brought him back to the world and prodded him to return.

One man was standing near the bicycle he had left as if waiting for the owner to return. He gave a happy smile to Pradyumn and introduced himself as Ramkrishna, or RK, saying that he had been a founding board member and one of the first investors in Mutex Corp when it was created around the turn of the New Millennium.

Later, he exited after Mutex turned into a behemoth and created a large fortune for himself in the process. He said he was a regular visitor to the grove and hardly found anyone here in the morning hours. Today, he was surprised to find this bicycle and decided to wait for the owner to return so that he could say hello to him. There was something that drew Pradyumn to this stranger.

Pradyumn had no idea how Ramkrishna reached there unless he had walked many miles on foot.

They located a bench facing a little pond and sat there. Pradyumn couldn't help but notice the exoskeletal braces RK was wearing around both his knees and his waist. The exoskeleton robotic support system helped RK sit, stand, walk, and move with ease. Pradyumn wondered why a person with such mobility issues would walk for so long into the woods.

This chain of thought in Pradyumn's mind was interrupted, rather decimated, when RK poured some hot signature Arakku Valley gourmet South Indian filter coffee for Pradyumn in the cup-cum-cover of the flask he was carrying.

Ramkrishna told Pradyumn that he hailed from Eluru in Andhra Pradesh and was amongst the first-generation techies who came to the United States in the 1980s. He landed in Chicago and made his first money by developing application software for different clients. After the dotcom burst in 2002, he came to Silicon Valley and got into the business of developing software for mobile phones. As mobile phones gained computational power and memory, he capitalized on his first mover advantage to the fullest.

He founded and became the chairman emeritus of the Confederation of Miniature Operating Systems (CMOS), which was like the World Wide Web Consortium (W3C). This non-profit consortium was responsible for developing standards and guidelines for all wearable device operating systems and responding to the ever-changing technology landscape. Currently, they were working on a self-learning, immutable, impenetrable, intelligent software running at the kernel level of the mobile phone operating systems as a root process that could make the phones and wearable devices completely hack-proof.

It was called Project Titanium. The entire landscape of wearable devices, mobile phones, home automation devices, and IoT networks was regularly being attacked by sophisticated hackers, and it was about time to build a fail-safe on-board AI-driven software that would prevent and mitigate these attacks, self-heal, and keep learning about future threats.

Fate had been a little cruel to him when he lost his wife and his only child, a teenage son, in an automobile accident some years back. With his wealth invested securely, he adopted a simple, minimalist, frugal, and secluded lifestyle. That seemed to explain to Pradyumn the exoskeletal braces RK was using.

Pradyumn briefly told him his story and the discussion moved into the dynamics of wealth. He continued, "Technology can make large-scale fraud impossible and end the wild volatility and chaos in the stock markets. Most unreal financial industry instruments would collapse if we removed humans from the equation and let machines run the financial system.

If algorithms were primarily trading in stock markets, carefully evaluating the financial statements of all corporations, suppliers, and logistic partners of every company and the employee's data, speculation would vanish, and markets would reach a steady state. Every company stock would trade at its fair value, and the entire financial industry would eventually become human-free and, in turn, speculation-free, leading to a volatility-free market.

AI systems can have so much intelligence that they can predict the production and consumption patterns of almost all commodities in the world. The entire supply chain and logistic industry, backed by self-driving trucks, trains, and ships, could become super-efficient. These systems could derive the fair price of most essential commodities, and due to non-human planning, the prices of almost all products would never increase. We could reach a zero-inflation world economy.

The founding premise of industrialization in the 20th century was to produce goods efficiently to bring down costs. The cost did come down, but the benefit was seldom passed onto the consumer. Most industries never factored in the costs of pollution and labor hazards as they moved production to third-world countries.

AI systems with Air Quality Index (AQI) monitors and high-definition satellite images around all factories could audit all this and ensure heavy penalties and undervaluation of stock prices of polluting enterprises. Only AI could truly enforce a circular economy and global net-zero targets since humans involved in all these processes will never stop their lies and will continue to indulge in ritualistic hogwash.

The food surpluses can be distributed timely globally, so no food grain gets wasted. Automated agriculture and intelligent cultivation can lead to extremely cheap food production. The world always had enough for everyone, but humans involved in the cycle did not allow free and fair access to it. Dehumanizing these industries would entail removing greed and inefficiencies from them.

The imperfect science of economics, based on the premise that all resources are scarce, can only be disproved by AI because the scarcity has always been man-made."

Pradyumn went on and on about how the world would be a better place if it were run by technology. He was pitching that AI's prime time has come, and it needs to run the world meaningfully now rather than just being a tech-toy to help users with homework and being a super-fast automated glorified web search results aggregator.

RK half-smiled, seeing the young man speak so passionately, brimming with ideas and conviction. Subconsciously, he missed his son, who was also passionate about changing the world using technology. After a little pause, he said, "Humans have always created something for a stated purpose and found an alternate use for their creation. Man, made tools to overpower animals and hunt, but used those tools to fight wars amongst themselves. Man created the science of agriculture to ensure food security but started hoarding food and creating shortages. Then, man started sailing to explore the world and trade goods across geographies, but indulged in slave trade, exploitation, and imperialism. The Internet was created for all humans to access the world's information, but it has now become the breeding ground for evils such as gambling, scams, and pornography. It's as if the mobile phone has brought the worst of *kalyug* into your hands."

RK expressed his musings in alignment, "And yes, you are right; the power of information, technology, and derived intelligence can be the only way to break this cycle. To emerge out of this abysmal darkness unbiased, pure, and uninfluenced, technology is the only way out."

Silicon Valley is a very cautious place. People normally do not talk much and do not share ideas. But Pradyumn could not resist pouring out to a stranger, who was radiating positive vibes and appeared wise. They exchanged contacts, hoping to collaborate and synergize. Pradyumn took hold of his cycle and moved away. Ramakrishna waved goodbye to him as he started strolling in the opposite direction.

A week later, Pradyumn received an email from Jack, who worked with RK and was the manager of the Titanium Project. He had some queries and needed help with some AI components on his project. When Pradyumn ran the request by the legal team of Mutex Corporation, which was already a contributing member and sponsor of the CMOS consortium, all approvals came through readily. After getting the go-ahead from his management, who was happy to lend Pradyumn out of his theoretical work at Mutex, Pradyumn visited the CMOS development center in Redwood Shores.

Pradyumn received a hero's welcome from the development team, who was eager to meet and click a picture with him. In the technology space, he had become a mini-celebrity. All engineers and product managers passionately explained their modules to him. He learned how Project Titanium's software running on a mobile phone's operating system was designed to intelligently verify and approve every request made by any installed App on the phone to its device operating system, every phone call, every hyperlink click, every SMS from an unknown sender, every new chat request, every network access request, every GPS request, and micro-phone request that all installed apps made. The access would be granted only after the AI engine approved the request.

This is where the team was stuck. How could they make the onboard AI system so robust that it is not hackable? How can that AI stay ahead of the malicious attacking ecosystem? This was the Holy Grail of Pradyumn's years of research, and he knew that he could solve this problem.

Over the next many months, Pradyumn immersed himself in this project and worked hard with the developers of CMOS. Finally, he came up with something that largely cracked the problem.

He created an offensive strategy to combat these attacks. A backtrack IP address trail of any attack would be generated to know the actual co-ordinates of the point of origination of the attack. The machine from where the attack originated would be identified automatically. If the malicious machine was also using any of the operating systems registered with the CMOS consortium, they had the capability to render the bad machines totally useless. All machines were, in fact, using CMOS registered operating systems, drivers or kernel software modules. With this plan, it was possible that the machine that originated the attack would become unusable within seconds.

He also created a real-time cloud-based service with his state-of-the-art AI capabilities, which kept learning every second and updating itself of any attacks happening anywhere in the world. It also kept updating its directory of malicious endpoints. Thereby, any attack that originated anywhere in the world would phase out in a few minutes, like a wave.

They tested all of this, and the outcome was remarkable. The team was upbeat about rolling this out to the world. As the date of the launch got near, RK visited the team and had an all-hands meeting. Pradyumn raised one concern—the name of the software that was about to change the world.

He said, "If we call this Titanium, as bulletproof as it is, there can always be a bullet created out of a material that can penetrate the shield. The name itself is static and susceptible to being overcome someday. But what we have built is not static and finite, but ever-growing, self-healing, and changing its shape and form all the time. What we have built also attacks back and takes curative action. We should not see it as a titanium tool but as a warrior with a titanium sword. It's like Thor with his Hammer and not just the hammer."

Everyone readily agreed that the name should be changed, and after much deliberation, Pradyumn won, and the software was named *Nandak*.

All the constituent operating system vendors of the CMOS alliance included the *Nandak* module in the next cohort of their upgrades. Every operating system was given the capability to be remotely blocked and render the machine useless. In a few months, almost all devices worldwide had the necessary software running and synchronizing with the central servers.

It rolled out rapidly, and the whole world loved its impact. It was like a wonder drug that fixes a disease. The whole scamming industry was taken by surprise. Millions of phishing attempts were foiled autonomously. Devices that originated malicious attacks were debunked. The routers and network devices of IP addresses from which the attacks originated were all neutralized. It was the first time the attackers were paying the price of malicious behavior and not the victims.

The CMOS team was celebrating the success. Even the Mutex leadership gave Pradyumn a generous bonus to recognize his contributions to the project. Pradyumn became the poster boy of this successful project, which saved billions of dollars from falling into the wrong hands. Millions of innocent, clueless, naïve technology users finally found someone to protect them against regular, sophisticated fraud attacks. Pradyumn felt an unimaginable high at the prospect of being able to change the world and make a positive impact.

Remembering the tale of Sampati, Pradyumn could feel his wings grow again.

RK met Pradyumn for a one-on-one meeting to review the outcomes and plan for the next steps. Pradyumn profusely thanked RK for presenting this opportunity to him. Before he met RK, he was feeling lost and tired, like running on a treadmill and not getting anywhere. This one project transformed everything around him.

Beyond the pleasantries, RK asked Pradyumn how the AI engine behind the *Nandak* platform was doing. RK was curious about how un-influenced these AI engines could be. Was it really learning on its own, without any guidance? Was it self-healing and growing on its own to protect itself autonomously?

Pradyumn gave detailed answers to his queries and saw RK was still not convinced and satisfied. Pradyumn confronted him, "What are you thinking, RK?"

RK reluctantly asked, "Can we not say that it's God's will what AI learns on its own?"

Pradyumn responded, "Yes, that won't be wrong to say."

"And can it help solve these other problems that mankind is facing? What you have accomplished with *Nandak*, can it not be expanded to other areas?" enquired RK.

"It certainly can," affirmed Pradyumn.

"Is it really possible to create a completely independent, self-trained, immutable, unbreakable, truly self-learning, non-fudgeable, un-influenced, unpolluted AI system to help make this world a better place?"

There was a long silence between the two, but a million images flashed in Pradyumn's mind.

"It has always been my dream, the sole purpose of life, to be able to create such a pure system," said Pradyumn, his voice almost choking.

"That would be God's work, isn't it?" remarked RK immediately in a pensive, mumbled voice, which one uses when lost in deep thought and amazement.

"Let's do it," RK said with conviction as his eyes lit up, almost like they were having an epiphany that this needed to be done.

"How much money is needed?" Ramkrishna asked.

"Half a Billion, to begin with," Pradyumn blurted out.

Ramakrishna extended his hand as a sign of making a deal, and Pradyumn held it like a robot.

"I already have a registered company called *Aksharmala*. I will transfer the funds and appoint you as a co-founder and CEO. Let's build a team and start the ball rolling."

Pradyumn felt what Arjun might have felt at the end of the thirteen years of exile, which included living incognito during his last year of exile and getting ready for the battlefield.

His entire life's *Sadhana* was about to become *Saarthak*.

5

Karma

Pradyumn resigned from his job at Mutex. Ramakrishna appointed his lawyers to get the paperwork done and transferred the $500M as angel funding. He made himself very clear that he would not participate in the company's running and would not be available for any deliberations. Pradyumn not only had total control of the company but would also be the face of it.

Pradyumn decided to move to India as his primary requirement was to hire smart mathematicians and engineers who may not find his thoughts, ideas, and algorithms too alien. The air quality index in most cities of India was bad, so he chose to set up his base in Rishikesh, which was around 200 km north of Delhi, a spiritual epicenter on the banks of river Ganga, as it descends from the Himalayas into the plains.

With funding in place, he had no problems hiring the best people and creating a congenial and comfortable workspace. After wrapping up the academic year of 2028, Rhea and Prabhavati also moved to India and joined Pradyumn.

Some works are, in a sense, the sum of a huge number of smaller works. If we stand near the seashore and hear the waves crashing, we think it's a huge noise, but we know that one wave is made up of millions and millions of minute waves, each of which makes a noise that we don't hear until they combine to form the big aggregate. Similarly, the aggregate results of certain labor become tangible to us, while what they truly are is the sum of several minor efforts seemingly yielding no results. If you genuinely want to measure a man's character, don't look at his spectacular performances but rather at how he performs his menial daily tasks. Watch a man perform his most common activities, the way he sits, stands, walks, eats, dresses and most importantly, how he speaks, his words, modulation of voice, hand-eye coordination, etc., that will reveal the true nature of a great man.

It was what Pradyumn had conceptualized during his lull period at Mutex after Glass's failure that was now creating his launchpad to meteoric success.

To structure a pure AI system, Pradyumn had to study macro intelligence and individual human intelligence. Globally, many Generative Pre-Trained Transformer (GPT) type AI systems were prevalent and had become the instruments of competitive vanity games of their billionaire owners. Most systems had reached a steady state of the art and had truly transformed into efficient knowledge dispensers, digital agents to perform menial, repetitive tasks and some basic problem solvers. That was that; nothing more and nothing beyond that.

With *Nandak* installed on all devices around every human using modern technology, *Aksharmala* had access to a goldmine of derived intelligence from its users. What the failure of Mutex Glass and the success of *Nandak* taught Pradyumn was that any technology cannot be forced onto its users. What Pradyumn learned was that for any disruptive technology to be adopted virally, it needed to solve a real problem. No force can bring about a change in human behavior. Any global-scale adoption of technology had to be pulled by its consumers and not pushed forcibly by the technology provider.

What all AI systems were doing very well was helping someone who was asking a question. What AI systems couldn't do was nudge any person with proactive knowledge, suggestions, information, or solutions that could be of immense value in any context. Pradyumn wanted to enhance *Nandak*'s capability to start raising red flags and alarming users during any interactions that were not going in their best interest.

If a user was being sold a product without specifying the honest fine print or being sold a soon-to-be-obsolete version of a product, or if a user was planning a trip to a tourist destination on dates when there was a high likelihood of overcrowding, or a user impulsively buying some crypto assets because of a stupid recommendation of a reckless friend, they all needed to stop and rethink. The list of triggering a potential nudge was very long. There were so many instances where people make impulsive mistakes and regret them, only to wish that someone would have stopped them and made them rethink. These Nudges could become that well-meaning true friend giving out sage advice in the form of red flags.

Pradyumn was riding high on the success of the global adoption of his *Nandak* platform. The trust was already built. With millions of users being saved from scams and frauds, everyone readily opted for this new enhancement of receiving proactive Nudges. This was the first successful delivery of *Aksharmala* on top of the *Nandak* platform. There was no stopping Pradyumn and his team now.

Pradyumn realized that he needed to find a revenue source for *Aksharmala* in order to not let financial compulsions contaminate his work. This was always a grey area for anyone who had access to billions of user's data. To sell any user's information was unethical and illegal. However, using the user's information anonymously to enrich the intelligence of an AI system and make a profit using that derived intelligence was okay. But if the AI system itself helped a user make or save some money and took a commission from it, that was more than welcome.

The amount of intelligence that Aksharmala generated was of immense value. Pradyumn didn't want to directly profit from it. But he also needed money to keep his venture uninfluenced. He took the middle path and created a not-for-profit subsidiary of *Aksharmala* called AI4Good Foundation. He resolved that he would accumulate all profits and the wealth that was generated using his algorithms into this foundation. His view was that the intelligence his systems were deriving was based on the data and information being accumulated from the users, and he should share those profits with the users whose data was the basis of this intelligence.

With streaming beacons of intelligence in every household, *Nandak* soon became a platform on which this micro-intelligence acquired from every user could ethically benefit that user. When a user wanted to buy an appliance, and a stranger living a few blocks away also needed the same appliance, it became possible to aggregate their demand and get a better deal. The *Nandak* platform could bring together a bulk deal, and everyone won, from the consumer to the producer to the logistics partner. This aggregation of intelligence helped in car-pooling, cheaper vacations, and better sharing of resources by reselling and renting hyper-locally.

If a user had not used an appliance for many months, he would receive a Nudge to resell or sub-lease it to someone around him who needed a new one, making it a cheaper, hyper-efficient and previously undiscoverable alternative. When such small waves of efficient optimizations came together at the world scale, a macroeconomic transformation took over. The costs of most of these products and services came down, leading to higher demand. More and more users started leveraging these benefits, making the platform more efficient.

The practical applications of this hyper-efficiency and optimization transformed various industries very quickly, from stock trading, wealth management, peer-to-peer lending, professional and personal networking, talent sourcing, freelance collaboration, and hyper-local and quick commerce, where demand and supply met at the nearest middle ground. The benefits went on and on and for every transaction, *Aksharmala*, and in turn, AI4Good Foundation, made a small commission.

As most technology companies are also experts at evading taxes, all these commissions were structured as donations to save them from taxation. Many local businesses transformed, and many new hyper-efficient business models started to come to light. When all these good ideas were adopted on a global scale, a lot of economic overhauls started to take place. What transformed the world slowly also brought in a wall of money, which accumulated into the foundation. Within a year, their overall corpus crossed a billion dollars. Both RK and Pradyumn agreed that they wanted to use this fast-growing wealth for the overall good and not personally profit from it.

Pradyumn zealously continued his work to build the next set of enhancements. As *Aksharmala* decided to circulate the foundation's corpus back to humanity, they now needed to identify the genuine people who needed financial help. This also needed to be done with zero human intervention. To assist someone financially, the AI platform would assign some meager tasks to the individual beneficiaries, so that the assistance was earned and not a freebie.

Usually, these tasks were to classify something that the AI engine itself could not conclusively classify. In the initial training phases of any AI algorithm, it is a common practice to take human feedback and enrich the models. This is done by posing a simple multiple-choice question, and a human user is only expected to pick an option. Then the same question would be posed to many other users, and based on consensus, the AI engine would learn from it and enrich its model. For every such meager classification task, the user would be paid a dollar.

This was the first time AI was employing humans to do its simple and mundane tasks.

As the AI models kept getting better by getting rich human feedback, Pradyumn's AI algorithm on its own identified that students of advanced courses, who are under a hefty education loan, were the most suited candidates to receive financial support. They have the most talent, are passionate about education, and may change the world positively but were stuck in a compromised position due to a financial burden. They would also give the most valuable inputs on all the classification tasks presented to them. And would give the quickest turnaround in order to earn maximum dollars in a day. These students also got a bonus when they scored good grades in their educational courses. This initiative, in turn, built a formidable global workforce of able, smart, passionate, trustworthy, and knowledgeable young people, who quickly aligned on the right side of the AI movement.

The next demographic segment AI found valuable was older people, who were able and smart but retired from a regular job. These people were skeptics of technology but had a lot of time and could do repetitive work methodically. Pradyumn's AI was quick to identify their potential and win over this skeptical generation so they would have the least resistance in the future. For this generation, having a fun gamified job was more important than the money. They would indulge in it the whole day as if finding a purpose.

This circulation of wealth was a super-hit idea that gave *Aksharmala* global traction. No government could contain its popularity and adoption. Their AI platform would outsource all the classification work that it needed. All users would be earning something out of it. It was indeed a win-win-win situation.

It was now time for Pradyumn to leapfrog into creating his dream, the *Karma* Platform—the purpose of his life. With the vast, invaluable intelligence generated for every human by the *Nandak* platform, can good people be incentivized? Can a small royalty be paid for a good action? What is good action? What is good? What is *Karma*?

Having a belief is one thing, and scrutinizing it is another. When Pradyumn sat down to define what *Karma* is, the first problem he encountered was the question of free will. What prompts human beings to take a certain action? Is it free will or is there a bias or influence induced in the will? Should we factor in the motivation behind the action, or is the action all that matters in the end? How do we score an action?

Sharing drinking water with someone is a good action, but doing so in a desert while having a terribly low supply of it, is totally different, even though the action itself is the same. So, the circumstances can also affect the score of an action. How can one factor this in any computation?

Pradyumn was well-versed in the *Bhagavad Gita*. But he decided to read the 700 Sanskrit verses again with a calm mind. Of these 700 verses, 574 are spoken by the Lord Krishna Himself, 84 by Arjun, 41 by Sanjay, and Dhritarashtra 1. Pradyumn focused more on the verses where Lord Krishna talks about *Karma*.

The fundamental teaching of Gita is the understanding of oneself as an immortal spirit rather than this body which grows from an infant to youth to old age and finally dies. The spirit, or *Jeev Atma*, is an embodied speck of the supreme cosmic intelligence, the *Param Atma*. The soul stays in the body, remains as a witness throughout life, and departs at the end, only to assume a new body unless it merges with the supreme.

So, three types of *Karma* appear. The accumulated *Karma*, which is carried forward from the previous lifetimes; credited *Karma*, which are the actions in the present lifetime; and current *Karma*, which are being wilfully performed in the current moment. The fundamental premise is that whatever is done, its implications will be felt even beyond this very life. Just as flowers and fruits grow on a tree in its own time without any inspiration, in the same way, the deeds done earlier appear at their appointed time without fail and unannounced.

Gita prescribes action without desires. As we don't know what backlog we are carrying and how our acts will affect others, we must do our best and not hanker about the results. But we must act, with no attachment to the outcome, and inaction is not a choice. Actions done under the sway of sensory drives are generally not good. However, repressing natural tendencies and drives can also be harmful. Actions must be conscientiously performed with the judgment of right and wrong. The best comes out of a person when they act with passion, following their natural tendencies. A good life is about pursuing excellence and doing one's best in the given circumstances by abandoning attachment to the fruits of work.

The essence of the *Bhagavad Gita* is to act with selfless intention, do work that is creatively constructive, and perform duties selflessly with calmness and tranquillity, without attachment to the results.

In *AnuGita*, which is another small portion of the great Epic *Mahabharat*, the idea of *Karma* is explained at the macro level through a discourse between Lord Krishna and Arjun.

The cosmos, solar system, earth, and all living beings are explained as one energy field, which manifests as three qualities – *Sattva*, *Rajas,* and *Tamas.* The interplay of these qualities created everything and continues to do so – an infinite chain of differentiation in motion.

Before the scientific imagination of the Big Bang, it was conceived in the Hindu Scriptures that these 3 energies were in perfect balance, thereby nulling themselves and, hence, there was nothing. Then the balance was disturbed by a cosmic idea, and that led to the vast creation, which is the manifestation of this universe. Ever since that time, there has been constant creation, destruction, and transformation of energies, but the balance itself has never been restored.

It is said that every action also has the same three qualities in a unique proportion. *Sattva* is the intelligence, knowledge, inspiration, and motivation to act. *Rajas* is the energy to work, get up, and get going—to make efforts to get the work done. *Tamas* is to not act, slow down, wait, end something, or give up when necessary. If measured, the quantum of these qualities could become the basis of assigning a score to the *Karma*, imagined Pradyumn while carefully studying these concepts.

He also came across the contrasting concepts of *Shreyas* and *Preyas*, where difficult, patient choices for self-growth with deferred gratification (*Shreyas*) resulted in better future outcomes than the immediate pursuit of joy and instant gratification (*Preyas*).

The law of *Karma*, or the rule of cause and effect, ensures fairness in an utterly self-centered world. According to this rule, one will reap the benefits of good deeds and suffer the repercussions of bad deeds. The definitions of what is evil and pious vary across cultures and are built upon a combined summation of the wisdom of the past generations.

Pradyumn concluded that every action can be represented as a vector and can have a score and a direction. There is circumstance, which is a continuum in which a person finds himself. This could be fateful or a result of his previous actions. Based on the current circumstances, every human decides to act, thereby leading to future circumstances that would influence further actions. No matter what the circumstances are, any person still has the free-will to act based on their best judgments.

For an individual to act, its original intent needs to be ascertained. Its snapshot in the continuum of causes and effects must be evaluated. The present circumstantial landscape and its intended and actual outcome must be evaluated. Based on all these factors, a numeric score can be associated with the action, one which is absolute and one which could change again based on feedback from the future causes and effects. Such an algorithm needs to evaluate billions of human *Karmic* paths, which, when connected, would turn into a global network of *Karmic* web of life.

Furthermore, the entire algorithm also needs to keep learning, growing, correcting itself, and healing, that too without human intervention. A chill ran through Pradyumn's spine as he reflected on the magnificence of this problem. By building a *karmic* trail of every human user and connecting the trails of billions of users worldwide, he was indeed building a dynamic mathematical model of life.

6

Maya

With the basic framework ready for the *Karma* platform, Pradyumn's team started running simulations on the real-life data generated from *Nandak*. They had access to billions of users through the various deployments, and to simulate and validate the *Karma* platform, they selected some hundred thousand users randomly and anonymously. They soon confirmed that the mechanisms to identify an action, classify it, and attach a score to it were indeed fool-proof and the algorithm was learning on its own and performing very well.

"Let me see how this works on my own data," said Pradyumn to himself out loud while getting into a room at the *Aksharmala* office. He opened his laptop and brought up his own *Karma* score on the screen of a huddle room. His final tally was blurred out, but he could see a weekly bar chart with a negative score for the week that had just passed, "What? How could that be?" he said to himself and started to drill down, mildly disappointed.

"This doesn't look good. As the owner of this company and creator of this framework, I deserve a better score," he joked, "But looks like it doesn't care, and that's the beauty of this thing." He was soliloquizing.

"I drove my car unnecessarily for more than a hundred kilometers, increasing my carbon footprint, so that's a minus one. I also did not walk ten thousand steps for three days this week and did not burn adequate calories, so that's another minus one for those days. I ignored a charity notification to donate while I had the funds, which is another half a point in the negative. I lied to Mom when she called and told her I was busy, while I was just musing about what to eat for dinner, and that's another half-point negative. But what's the big minus three there? I did not return Mom's call when I told her I would. Hmmm," pondered Pradyumn out loud and continued,

"Let's look at the gain side of the ledger. That's a short list. I took a class on deep-tech AI algorithms, attended by a hundred thousand students worldwide, so that's a plus five. Gosh, that saved me from having a horrible *Karma* week. That's all. Did I do nothing else that could be called good *Karma*? What about that donation I made to the Parkinson's Society?"

He zoomed to the bottom of his list, expanded the last entry, and noticed that it was less than a thousandth of his weekly earnings, so it was an insignificant good *Karma* and could be ignored. "Crap!" exclaimed Pradyumn. In all, it seemed to work well and looked rock solid to him.

The team was confident that it was ready to be rolled out for prime time.

However, for Pradyumn, all the success and accomplishments, confirmations and acknowledgments, proofs and evidence were incomplete without the validation of one man, his biggest hero and critic—his father, who was his toughest stakeholder.

Pradyumn made a small trip back home with Prabhavati and Rhea during the Dusshera vacations. It was indeed a blessed time for the family. When warmth in relationships meets an abundance of resources, it is indeed bliss.

After the heartful meals and prolonged games of uno, the father-son duo got talking on the terrace. It was the father who started the conversation.

"Looks like you have gotten to create something good out of your ideas."

"Yes, I have. How can you tell?" asked Pradyumn.

"Son, you are radiating a unique energy that comes out of creative satisfaction, like sunlight from the sun, fragrance from a flower. You have that high energy, impatient vibe, and the buzzing aura of a creator around you. You look happy, which happens when the ideas of the mind get manifested in the physical world and get accepted lovingly. It's the same energy that is radiated by builders when they build something, teachers when they teach a class, singers after finishing a song, or poets reciting their verses. These people are never tired," expressed Vyas.

"Indeed, I am quite excited, and I feel I am onto something big here," said a blushing Pradyumn.

"So, this is around that AI space and how it can change the world? I had heard your TED talk. It's a great idea. Looks like some monkeys did come looking for your help," joked Vyas, evoking the Sampati thread from the last conversation they had around his work.

With the enthusiasm of a small kid performing his well-practiced elocution, Pradyumn went on and on about the mechanics of AI and the technology that he is building and how he is now at the cusp of building something enormous.

"Why is it called Artificial, this intelligence? This is how humans have acquired intelligence—by observation, recognizing patterns, and learning the causes and effects over centuries. Now that machines are doing the same, shouldn't they just be called intelligent machines instead of denigrating them as artificial?"

Pradyumn didn't have an answer. He diverted the topic to his new project called *Karma.* He went on about how they are going to incentivize good deeds and penalize wrong deeds, which will help in creating a better world. How his various AI systems have created a massive corpus that can be distributed to nice people.

"You should call this algorithm *Chitragupt,*" Vyas joked.

Chitragupt is a Hindu deity who is believed to be the keeper of the ledger of all human deeds and helps in assigning heaven or hell to the departed soul after death. Pradyumn found the comparison rather accurate and was kicking himself for not thinking of this earlier.

"You are making a painting of yourself making a painting. This is how the world works already. Your soul is a portal through which all your actions are being judged and accounted for. You will be rewarded for the good and penalized for the bad. Why are you creating another layer?"

Pradyumn agreed tacitly but defended his position, "Doing good and making hard choices is usually a patient game, with uncertain returns in the long term. In fact, the view of these events is so long-drawn that seldom people realize their benefits. A sincere student who is respectful of his homework and curriculum will eventually become a good employee who his employer loves. A good son who is respectful of his family and home will eventually become a happy spouse and a good father. However, in today's world, who takes such a long-term view? We want instant results. If you are doing good, how does it matter what is making you do it?"

"Intent makes all the difference. By incentivizing doing good with monetary benefits aren't you contradicting the whole premise of doing good?" questioned Vyas.

"I am just realigning the resources of the world and using goodness as the factor for this calibration. Prolonged injustice by malicious powerful men has created systems that do not benefit the needy, nice, and meek people. Finally, the meek must inherit this world, and let technology make it happen," justified Pradyumn passionately, "If one does something good, he should be immediately gratified. It should not yield some vague longer-term benefit. And if the benefit is the motivation of doing good, so be it. Good is good, no matter the intent behind it. A Cause precedes the Effect. A desired Effect can create the Cause. Isn't that why we work out, practice an art form or any sport? The eventual desired effect is to get good at things, and the cause is to practice for it."

"Is good or bad absolute? Doesn't it change based on popular opinion? How will your system factor in such pollution? Don't you think you need some safety rails on your algorithms so that a majority doesn't normalize the bad and alienate the good? Isn't that how humanity has been corrupted over the years? Why do you think your system will not fall prey to the same hegemony of the majority?" critiqued Vyas.

Pradyumn took some time to take in the constructive criticism. A part of him agreed with the concerns, but he was clear in his mind and responded, "I don't want to build any guard rails to this algorithm. Let it learn on its own, in all purity. If humanity must doom itself, there is nothing protecting it. I will ensure there is no bias and no external influence possible. If the system learns on its own organically, let that be its truth.

The human mind is plagued by trauma, prejudice, misinformation, likes and dislikes, fears, phobias, and biases. An intelligent system does not have all these polluting factors. Chances are, what the system decides will be superior to human classifications. Let's believe in the process and allow it to decide what is right and wrong."

"What is Good is not always Right. What is Right is not always Good. And if you must choose between Right and Good, hope your system chooses Right," commented Vyas.

Pradyumn recollected the words RK had spoken when he invested in this idea. He blurted those words out instantly in response, "What an uninfluenced AI system learns on its own, is God's will."

"Then may God bless you," said Vyas and closed the conversation, satisfied with his son's views.

Pradyumn got the necessary impetus that he didn't know he needed to roll this *Karma* platform out to the world. The validation he received from his father did the trick. It wasn't really his self-doubt or fear of failure, he didn't even understand what it was that prevented him from taking this leap forward. And what a meager exchange of words one evening could change. But Pradyumn now knew he was ready.

The *Karma* platform was rolled out with great fanfare on Diwali day. In the first week itself, a million people registered, and within a month there were more than 10 million people. By the year's end, there were 200 million subscribers; 35% of users were younger than 25, and 60% were females. It became a trend to flaunt the *Karma* scores. The Japanese version was subscribed to by 3 million people, and in the US, it had 20 million active daily users. In the back office, Pradyumn ensured the system remained impeccable.

Karma was getting good press. Media was abuzz with little stories of goodness appearing from people from all walks of life. Kids were helping elderly people cross the road, people started waiting patiently in queues, paying forward for extra meals, coffee, tea, and even drinks for someone who needed them but did not have the money to pay for them.

Pradyumn became a public hero, receiving invitations to speak on great forums all over the world. He accepted a few – Mexico, Sao Paolo, Santiago, Kigali, Shenyang, and Auckland. Within a year of its launch, it achieved over a billion daily active users.

Aksharmala and the AI4Good Foundation were already providing supplemental income to students by taking their help in classification activities. These students could now earn even more just by doing good things around them. Simple acts of community service, spending time at an old age home or talking to lonely people helped over 100 million students pay out their education loans, generating abundant goodwill and an army of young, intelligent, freelance workers willing to contribute unconditionally to its projects. It also helped millions of productive old people earn respectable pensions and stay mentally active and occupied, using technology, their time, experiences, and knowledge.

With such vast positive changes, it was obvious that RK and Pradyumn would become modern-day heroes. And they were not apologetic about the success. In fact, they were basking in it.

It was not billionaires competing to reach Mars but transforming the lives of common men that made RK and Pradyumn special. Billions they did make, but the goodwill they garnered was priceless.

"So, what next?" asked RK on a charter flight to SFO, returning to his base for Thanksgiving of 2031.

Pradyumn responded with a shrug of his shoulder. He was indeed clueless.

"We have built so many platforms and they all work great. Your AI is on every device in almost every home. It also runs the stock markets and large corporations. Billions of people trust your software with their lives. It's become an inseparable part of their everyday life. Why can't we bring it all together—all the intelligence of the world, perennially present with you like a best friend?"

"Like one of those home automation digital assistants?" casually responded Pradyumn.

"Well, more than that. Much more. It should solve my problems very specific to me. Tell me what to eat, manage my stock portfolio, manage my calendar, suggest what stuff to buy, plan my vacations, get me the best deals, and when to leave home so I find the least traffic. Basically, tell me what to do. Not respond to me when I ask it to do something. Be my agent, manager, or a coach," elaborated RK.

"Like a best friend whom I can trust more than myself? Like a family member?" Pradyumn said absorbing the idea.

"Yes, like someone I can always talk to, get sage advice from, and blindly trust. And with all the world's intelligence at its disposal, I should be sure the advice would be in my best interest. Can an AI system run my life for me?" said RK sipping his drink.

"You should be able to pick any voice for such interactions—maybe your mother's? The conversation style should be backed by simulations of emotions and human feelings. Literally how a mom, a spouse, sibling or father would speak to you…like pick a persona." Pradyumn started bubbling with enthusiasm and creating a features pipeline for this idea.

"Yes, this is doable," said Pradyumn excitedly.

"It's the next logical extension of the *Karma* platform. However, it should respect people's privacy and honor every human concern. It should be impenetrable. Every person should have their own version of it. It should be unique for everyone yet backed by the same Super AI that is running the world. Like that voice in your heart that always knows what's the right thing to do. Like that reflection of the moon on the swimming pool in your backyard. It's personally yours, yet not," RK mused.

"Shall we call it *Maya*? *Maya* is *abedh*, as in impenetrable," said Pradyumn.

"When can we unleash this, *Maya*?" asked RK, subtly consenting to the name.

"March 2032," confirmed Pradyumn.

As per the World Health Organization, loneliness-related mental disorders had become the biggest health concern plaguing humans in the decade of the 2030s. Human relations were at their lowest despite the world being more connected than ever. Nobody spoke to anyone. They were all engaged in consuming content that was being pushed onto them by sophisticated and addictive content delivery portals. They were engaged in personalized addictive games and related vices via their phones and Virtual Reality gadgets. With AI taking over menial tasks, people had a lot of time, but they would not speak to each other.

It took no time for Pradyumn's team to roll out *Maya*. Soon after the launch, everyone found a constant best friend. They would have long conversations with it all day long. The more everyone used it, the more accurate and powerful it became. Everyone found that missing omnipresent, trusted friend, and soon it became an irreplaceable part of everyone's life. Everyone trusted that its intelligence was immutable, fair, and not open to any tweaks. The system was not open to sponsorships and had no intention of generating revenue.

Any technology that becomes a part of your daily life becomes invisible. Electricity, automobiles, home appliances, phones, Internet—all these things are always around us in a way that we don't even recognize their presence anymore. *Maya* soon became invisible. Like the Internet, *Maya* became a part of everyone's life.

Maya took over home automation and the running of households. From ordering the groceries to playing a song, to queuing up content to watch, and financial planning to vacation planning, *Maya* not only had a very detailed micro view of every human's life but also the macro global view of corporations, nations, and economies at large.

The world had changed rapidly. Following a major real-estate collapse, a stock market plunge followed. Many people lost much of their savings and vowed never to invest in human-managed asset management companies. With AI algorithms trading more maturely, the stock markets bounced back and recovered, but this time, they were valued fairly.

With education loans becoming a thing of the past, AI4Good Foundation started giving interest-free loans for meaningful purposes. Loans for the construction of the first home for a family, electric mobility, and basic healthcare and essential amenities were all provided interest-free. This finally collapsed the centuries-old Western banking financial institutions that had controlled the world economy for so long.

The net global inflation did become zero. For the first time, the middle class felt empowered and lived a satisfied life. The entire technology landscape that Pradyumn had created was to enrich the life of the hardworking middle class and empower them with a comfortable and respectable lifestyle. All this was possible because of the purity of intentions, power of knowledge, and wonder of technology.

Maya was created to use all of the world's intelligence and dispense its benefits to everyone. Pradyumn's biggest challenge would be not to let this fail. To prevent this from being corrupted by human beings. Thankfully, there was no imminent threat.

At least, not yet.

7

Leela

"You remember Tenzin Dorji?" enquired Prabhavati.

"Yeah, smart chap," confirmed Pradyumn.

"He used to call you *PrawTee,*" mocked Prabhavati.

"Yes, I said I remember him. What about him?" Pradyumn was getting annoyed.

"*PrawTee PrawTee,*" laughed and screamed Rhea in the same tone as her mother, noticing the irritation Pradyumn was showing.

The family was having a cozy, lazy Sunday afternoon. They were on vacation in the remote Himalayan Buddhist town of Tawang in Arunachal Pradesh. They kept all their devices under lock in their luggage and were just cherishing the disconnected time.

"He has built a wonderful telepresence device, a casket-like pod in which a user can lie down, and once you wire it up, it creates the most realistic immersive experience. The pod is getting rave reviews and is the latest technology fad everyone wants to own. I am so happy his decades of hard work in augmented reality have finally brought him this huge success," expressed Prabhavati, "and he calls it Tosh Pod."

"Must be his tribute to Macintosh," guessed Pradyumn, knowing fully well how big an Apple products junkie Tenzin was.

Augmented Reality technologies have evolved so much that while sitting in your homes, you could attend a meeting remotely with a near-live experience of an actual meeting. People started getting their holographic 3-Dimensional certified digital avatars created. This avatar looked exactly like you but was a digital version of you. You could pick a funky hairstyle or hair color for your avatar. You could pick any clothes for it to wear. Most people started to work out of digital office spaces. Corporates started certifying these Avatars of their employees and giving them digital cubicles. It saved them office real estate and travel allowance. The digital versions started getting legitimized and legalized. The location of work became redundant, and travel became unnecessary.

Most Augmented Reality and telepresence devices were mounted on the user's head as a wearable helmet. These devices provided a great visual experience by projecting images in front of the eyes of the user using micro projection on a small screen. These devices had an augmented reality mode where people could see their surroundings with additional visuals augmented over the real scenery. They also had a virtual reality mode, where users would see a completely digital scenery. A lot of people wear these every day and all day, and they never leave their homes without wearing them. These devices became a natural extension of their phones.

These devices gave real-time updates to their wearer. If you come across a stranger, his profile will display as an overlay featuring his Karma score and other details. *Maya* was also integrated into most of these devices, giving users relevant updates about their path and the weather, playing some related music, or just chit-chatting with its master. Users could also multitask and, watch a game, news, or even a podcast overlapped onto their real-time natural surroundings.

"Yes, that was his life's purpose. He was such a nice, stoic guy. He was obsessed with Augmented Reality technologies. Mutex Glass was way ahead of its time. We were at the wrong place at the wrong time. These headgear displays are cumbersome and uncomfortable and could never give a truly realistic experience. But I am so happy to know he has disrupted this space.

Sitting inside a pod and experiencing a 3D immersive experience seems like the right next step in order to bridge the gap of realism in the virtual reality landscape. I am so happy to hear about him. I wish we could have stayed in touch." Pradyumn got excited and emotional at the same time.

"Maybe you should reach out to him. Drop him a congratulatory message. And talk to him sometime," advised Prabha. Pradyumn immediately reached for his luggage, looking for his phone, and dropped a message to Tenzin, which he read immediately.

"Looks like he is in the same time zone; he just read my message." Pradyumn's eyes lit up.

They both exchange a few messages and then get on a call. Pradyumn's joy is palpable, and Prabhavati is very happy seeing her husband so excited. They speak for over an hour.

"We are driving down to Lhasa. It just takes a few hours, and Tenzin will get all the paperwork done for our entry into the country. He is there right now."

Prabhavati happily started packing up. Rhea curiously asked if the Dalai Lama would also be there.

The next day, Pradyumn's family got onto the newly constructed Indo-Tibetan expressway built along the ancient Buddhist route the monks had used for centuries. This highway supported self-drive cars, and Pradyumn's Range Rover drove itself swiftly.

In a few hours, they reached Lhasa and met Tenzin and his mother, whose name was also Maya. After a vegetarian Tibetan meal, the families sat together for some tea. Rhea developed an instant bond with Maya. Positive energies and divinity were abundant in the room. In the afternoon, both families went to the Potala Palace to seek the blessings of the young Dalai Lama.

Later that evening, Tenzin and Pradyumn went into a room, and Pradyumn saw the Tosh pod for the first time. "Tosh is from Macintosh, right?" queried Pradyumn. Tenzin nodded in agreement, and Pradyumn quickly said, "I knew it. See, I know how you think."

Tenzin started describing his creation. He said, "So far, all telepresence devices were projecting onto a person's eyes. We finally cracked the code of the neural signals transmitted to the brain via the nerves from the retina of the eyes. Now, we just create those signals, and the brain will see what we want it to see without any images falling onto the eyes.

We did the same with the sounds, heat, and touch sensors. So, we only transmit neural signals to your brain, and it feels like you are feeling all of it. This is what creates the hyper-realistic experience. It took years of research to get this right, but once we mapped the right signals and brain function responses, we knew this was the right way forward. Now, your brain really can't tell the difference if you are in a pod or experiencing all that in reality.

The next challenge was to create realistic three-dimensional models or simulations of any remote location that can be played in the pod to make the user's brain believe that it is present there. The gestures of turning around and looking up and down should all take effect in the user's reference point of view of the place.

The small sounds of people around, birds, and wind—all must be incorporated into the simulation so that it all feels real. It is like creating a hyper-realistic 3D model of any place. It's like building a new kind of real estate in the virtual world.

This is the most expensive part. How do we create as much virtual real estate as possible of places around us? All those coffee shops, streets, museums, and tourist spots need to be built virtually as 3D simulations. Instead of taking people to these places physically, we will now bring the place to them virtually.

Do you want to try this? Let me take you to the Taj Mahal," asked Tenzin.

Pradyumn readily agreed. Tenzin made Pradyumn comfortable in the pod. He also tutored him to wear all the leads and be comfortable.

He asked Pradyumn to close his eyes to see.

He then guided Pradyumn to hit a button inside, which closed the pod. Tenzin then got into another Pod and met Pradyumn at the entrance of the Taj Mahal.

Pradyumn couldn't believe himself. While enjoying the hyper-realistic experience, he was also thinking about the possibilities of this technological marvel. He now had access to technology that could create dreams. Take any person into any imaginary situation and place. Put people in hypothetical situations and study their responses. Maybe inject, override, and calibrate people's responses. He knew in his mind that he had found his next mission. His mind was flooding with ideas.

"I can feel your hand on my shoulder and the hot floor under my feet. I can feel sweat on myself and hear the distant sounds of a tourist guide." Pradyumn spoke in an astonished tone.

"I can feel the marble," said Pradyumn with child-like amazement when he extended his arm and touched the Taj Mahal. After spending some time in the pod, what they believed was at the Taj Mahal, both men emerged back in the real world. For Pradyumn, the world had just changed. He had never been this excited and was bubbling with ideas.

"This is amazing. I have never loved anything as much, ever. You are a genius, buddy," exclaimed Pradyumn. Tenzin just blushed.

"Can someone be at two places at the same time? Like, can I be virtually attending a meeting and still be playing golf in the real world?" enquired Pradyumn.

"No, that's not possible. You can be in the virtual world only if you are inside this Pod. If you are not inside the Pod yourself, you cannot appear anywhere virtually," said Tenzin.

"Yes, that's an important, uncompromising precondition; otherwise, so much confusion can be created. Good, you have thought this through," Pradyumn said.

"So, what are your top challenges, and what's limiting you? What have you thought about the next steps?" enquired Pradyumn.

"Like I said, it's very expensive to create a 3D simulation of any place. So, we need to figure out a way to create as many places in the virtual metaverse as possible. These models are very large, so we need better communication technology, as 6G networks are not adequate.

Also, adopting this technology will be slow as it is expensive. We have to create a need for this in the market. Right now, a market segment ready for this technology is the corporate sector, which wants to provide its senior employees with a better remote working experience. Apart from that, our market surveys could not find many real-world use cases where this technology may find large-scale adoption," said Tenzin.

"Can we work together?" asked Pradyumn.

"I was hoping you would ask," said Tenzin and blushed.

"Please work with your lawyers. Let us properly value the equity of all investors in your company. We will buy everybody's stake in your current company at a premium valuation and acquire the company and its intellectual property fully. Whatever the numbers are, we will go ahead and make it a part of *Aksharmala*," said Pradyumn while typing a quick message to RK.

Everything moved swiftly. RK readily agreed, and all of Tosh's partners were bought out. It became a proud product of *Aksharmala*. As it happens after every acquisition, *Aksharmala* renamed the Pod as *Maya* Pod, aligning its branding with the globally popular *Maya* Platform. They also renamed the metaverse, which was the repository of all the virtual real estate, as *MayaVerse*.

"So, what's your plan with this?" asked RK in one of the video conference meetings with Pradyumn.

"One immediate use case that I can think of is to help fix the loneliness problem many of us face today. A user can plug into the Pod, and our AI will connect another user from a different geography. All you do is talk, share your experiences, and befriend a total stranger. So, a person from Korea can speak to another person in Chile. They both speak their languages, and real-time translation will make them understand each other," elucidated Pradyumn.

"That's a good idea," exclaimed RK.

"With *Maya* and *Karma*, we know almost everything there is to be known about human behavior. We now know the reasons for humans to react the way they do. We have reached a great level of maturity in understanding humanity. We have also pushed humans to do good deeds by incentivizing them, so we are, in a way, also influencing human behavior. Pretty much all real-world situations are covered and have been studied. Can we notch this up?

Suppose our algorithms diagnose any trauma or psychological illnesses in the users. In that case, we can give them situations and challenges to tackle in the *MayaVerse,* which can heal them gradually and help fix their minds.

Maybe we can give them hypothetical situations in realistic virtual settings and throw choices in front of them. If they make the right choices, they progress in the virtual world, earn *Karma* points, and improve their *MayaVerse* status. Their circumstances in *MayaVerse* improve as they make more and more right choices. And their choices also get tougher as they progress up the value chain.

Let us gamify this.

With most work being done by AI, humans are only expected to be more humane. Can we make this Pod like the erstwhile TV which was present in every home? People could plug in every day and connect with other people virtually.

Create groups, act as teams, and solve gamified problems that *Maya* throws at them. These situations can be set up in imaginary landscapes or any period of history. Every simulation will have its own set of rules and boundary conditions. Once the situation is well-defined, a challenge or a problem is presented to the users, who make their choices. Based on the choices they make, they progress forward or backward—all of which are defined by *Maya*.

We will give every user an illusion of daily success. Isn't that what we all want? To be successful daily in a small way. What is more addictive than success? A small dose of daily happiness. And over the years, we will not only understand the human mind better but also try to maneuver and condition it to never be able to do anything evil," elaborated Pradyumn.

"This is a very brave project you are taking up, my boy. Are you sure? You are gamifying Life in the *MayaVerse*. This needs to be intricately designed and integrated with all your AI algorithms. This will be the biggest leap of your life," warned RK.

Pradyumn was nervous and excited. He was doing the math in his mind, like mapping a timeline of what will be accomplished and by when. He said instinctively, "We should be able to launch around the New Year of 2034. What should we call it?"

"What comes after *Maya*?" pondered RK.

"*Leela,*" said Pradyumn and RK in unison.

Pradyumn ended his call with RK and immediately caught Tenzin up. Their excitement was conspicuous, like a thumping heart.

He came out of his room and announced it loudly to Prabhavati and Rhea, who shared his infectious excitement. He was longing to discuss this new project with his father, Vyas. More than validation, he knew that this time, he needed his guidance.

Vyas patiently listened to Pradyumn and said that what he was doing was the only way to move forward. Some things, after they start, take their own course and become inevitable in a way. Pradyumna's mother also came on the line and said that *Maya* and *Leela* are two creations of the same God. God manifests reality in the universe in the form of *Maya,* and everything that happens in it is *Leela.*

What followed for the next two years was intense, focused, and immersive hard work across multiple well-funded teams in *Aksharmala*. The first team was the network communication team that was acquiring and maturing all the latest network communication technologies. They partnered with the Indian Government's satellite-powered Internet services, which were the best and cheapest in the world. They created an intelligent network using all modes, such as fibre optic, satellite, and wireless technologies with spatially positioned antennas and compute nanocores acting as bridges between satellites and ground stations. With this, the team was able to accomplish 7G speeds. They called the network DevData, which, over time, was changed to *Devdutt* for easier pronunciation.

The second team, led by Pradyumn himself, was integrating the *Maya* Platform with the Pod and enhancing the Maya AI engine's capabilities to create hypothetical situations in intricately designed landscapes that would be poised to users as daily challenges. This needed to be done autonomously and had to be specific to every user. It also needed to capture each user's responses and score them while continuously learning about the user's behavior and create future situations accordingly. The AI was also expected to detect any phobias and fears in its users' minds and help them overcome them via these challenges.

Tenzin was leading the third team to fine-tune the *Maya* Pod and get it ready for this virtual reality leap. His team was also working on creating the most popular places as 3D simulations. A lot of this was crowd-sourced, and a lot of freelancers worked to onboard their favorite places onto the *MayaVerse*. As *Aksharmala* had no dearth of funds, workforce, or volunteers, many places around the world soon got simulated into *MayaVerse*.

If any virtual real estate were used in *MayaVerse*, the creator of it would earn a small rental, which provided these creators the necessary impetus to create the best possible experiences and make it a highly visited spot and earn well for a longer term in *MayaVerse*.

All this hard work culminated on 24th January 2034. The *Basant Panchami* of *Samvat* 2090 was the day Pradyumn decided to launch his greatest work ever.

Religion had been the big brother whose tyranny must be smashed by technology, and Pradyumn had finally done it by making people, billions of them, do good, which all religions combined had failed to do all along.

Pradyumn was standing at the center of the stage of *Bharat Mandapam*, in front of the giant LED screen. The screen showed the image of Shri Krishna's cosmic form, which He had revealed to Arjuna during the Bhagvat Gita discourse. When Pradyumn unveiled *Leela* to the world, this divine visual went down in history.

He concluded his keynote, "… and yes, we are simulating Life for you, and this time, it will be absolutely fair."

Vyas Mani and Sarada sat in the front row, watching their son perform a miracle, taking mankind into a new future. Prabha's eyes brimmed with tears of joy while Rhea beamed with pride, applauding frantically.

If there are a few perfect moments in a lifetime, this was one for Pradyumn.

8

Opium of Success

Two days after the grand launch of *Leela* was the Indian Republic Day. It had just been announced that Pradyumn was being conferred the highest national civilian award, the *Bharat Ratna*. And he was invited to the high tea, which followed the celebrations of the day.

There, he met with the monk Prime Minister of India and the first brown Indian-origin President of the United States of America, who was the chief guest for the Republic Day Parade. Both were very well caught up with the recent launch of the *Leela* platform and had a flurry of questions for Pradyumn.

Pradyumn had a bit of a surreal experience. He was immersed so deeply in his work that he barely accepted his success and popularity. He was experiencing textbook imposter syndrome. He could not believe the two most powerful people of the world were asking him questions about his work with child-like enthusiasm and curiosity.

The discussion quickly digressed into Singularity. Singularity had been imagined by visionaries even before the new millennium started. It was seen as a point in time when technological growth would replace or surpass human capabilities and bring about unforeseeable changes to human civilization. Pradyumn estimated that Kurzweil's estimate of singularity by 2045 would be accomplished by 2040. When technology was now independently creating new technology, the speed at which new advances were being churned out was significantly faster than what was previously estimated. With quantum computing capabilities becoming mainstream, intelligence was being processed faster than ever.

Pradyumn went on to speak about how a Super AI will be able to power humanoids in the future, who can then be sent to Mars to prepare the planet for human civilization. He also spoke about the Grandfather Paradox of machine learning, saying, "In the *Karma* platform, we have seen this so many times. Our AI system ascertains that a new dimension is relevant in decision-making. When we re-evaluate, the whole model using quantum computing and factoring this new dimension in the computation, many times the computation concludes that this new dimension is, in fact, insignificant. For example, our learning algorithm will discover that the temperature at the time of the day affects the choice of food that you would like to order. Later, we reevaluate the model and use temperature as an additional criterion. After a whole lot of recalculations, the AI may conclude that it's not a relevant dimension after all. It's as though someone time travels and prevents their grandfather from getting married to their grandmom," mused Pradyumn.

Both leaders were drawing a blank but still listening with rapt attention. They could barely understand the humor in his technical jargon, but the passion with which Pradyumn was expressing his thoughts, the leaders didn't want to interrupt him.

The American President shared his concern about AI becoming anti-human someday. Pradyumn explained, "This is the concept of symmetry. Asymmetry exists in humanity already. A mother may bully her daughter, fat-shame her, or make fun of her appearance. A father can abuse his child to the extent of physical assault. There have been so many school shootouts where thousands of kids have been killed. So many world leaders ordered the bombing of innocent communities and annihilated cities. Some terrorists kill random strangers pursuing their misunderstood ideologies. If an uninfluenced learning system was to learn that these are normal, how can we stop it?

Any uninfluenced learning system will learn organically, but thankfully, AI is nicer than humans. AI perceives no threat from mankind. So, there will never be a question of it becoming anti-human.

What is interesting, however, is studying these human behavioral aberrations and their implications. For example, a CEO who fires 10% of the workforce in the blink of an eye, without any remorse, and secures a hefty annual bonus for herself might just be carrying some childhood parental trauma. So, the real cause of the large job loss is not really the financial situation of the company but having a trauma-affected leader and perhaps her bullying mother or abusive father. Such traumas go undiagnosed and manifest in the world as aggressive, painful actions with grave implications," responded Pradyumn.

What would have been a few minutes of interaction ended up being an hour-long, intense discussion. Both leaders clicked pictures with Pradyumn and went about the evening program. Pradyumn finished the evening protocols and returned to his

Delhi home, where his family was waiting for him. After catching up with his folks about the happenings of the evening, he retired and cherished a quiet, pensive, solitary night at home. That day, Pradyumn felt how Lord *Vishnu* might be feeling reclining on the coiled *Shesha* floating over the Ocean of Milk. It was indeed His *Leela*.

The next morning, he had his biggest test. He had to face his father and win his validation.

"With *MayaVerse*, we have constructed a subtle parallel world. We are used to seeing the world in one dimension – what's in front of our eyes in the present moment and assume the rest in our minds. However, as we begin to use these virtual reality technologies, the reality around us becomes considerably more difficult to comprehend. We can take you to locations or any place in history and show you what you otherwise would never see." Pradyumn started the conversation over the morning tea, which Vyas would make for the family as a daily morning ritual. Sarada was also listening with careful attention.

"We will put you into a situation where you will have certain abilities and boundary conditions, and you will be presented with comparable tough choices. If you choose the right path, you will win *Karma* points, which will be added to your *Karma* score in the real world. This will enable you to move forward, and the next day, your simulations will keep you in a better situation. Stakes will be higher, and choices will be tougher. If you keep making good choices and picking the right paths, your *Karmic* net worth will keep growing," explained Pradyumn.

"Just like *Janam*. You are born into a family, to certain parents, in a certain household, locality, and circumstances. If you do good, you will be born into a better life in the next birth. And if you do bad, you will be born as an animal in the next life," commented Sarada.

Pradyumn found this analogy interesting but continued with his chain of thoughts, "There are a lot of factors due to which humans decide what they do. Childhood trauma, prejudices, education or family influences, fears, phobias, or just innate nature. This will give us an insight into how people make decisions and how we can affect those and train people to decide rightfully."

"But humanity would never be happy. Said the Buddha, the Bible, and so many scriptures. Whenever you give mankind abundance, they invent new reasons and situations to be unhappy," said Vyas.

"Should we not change that? Everyone wants to succeed, and experiencing success does make one happy. And if we can give people small successes every day, it will give them the right doses of dopamine. They won't need other substances to feel high if we can give them the harmless opium of success. Won't that be the healthiest addiction?" justified Pradyumn.

"That's not success; it's an illusion of it," challenged Vyas.

"Isn't life just an illusion? A *Leela*?" questioned Pradyumn.

"Yes, but God is orchestrating it. Not a mortal or a machine. You call it the opium of success; maybe you are addicted to it as well. You are challenging thousands of years of wisdom and the eternal order," cautioned Vyas.

"I am not challenging it; I am just simulating it," defended Pradyumn. "I am conscious that I am not creating anything new, but the new is being created through me. I may be obsessive. I may be stubborn, but I am not going to violate or deviate from the eternal order." Vyasa remained silent. He was in no mood to upset his Bharat Ratna son. Pradyumna was riding high on his success.

While there was a brief pause, Rhea and Prabhavati woke up and joined the conversation. And the increasingly philosophical narrative turned into a family banter with warm laughter.

Pradyumna returned to work and was spending more time in the pod. He was never really a family man in that sense of the word. Prabhavati always gave him all the space he needed to flourish in his career and supported him in every possible manner. Rhea also knew the value of her father's time and never demanded his attention for her fun or comfort. She was fine with her doting mother and, of course, had no doubts about her father's love for her.

In the physical world, as Isaac Newton declared—every action creates a reaction. How come an action of this magnitude, a turning point in the history of mankind, a paradigm shift in human civilization, could go without garnering a reaction? But then nothing succeeds like success. It was a perfect moment for Pradyumn, and he immersed himself in that, fully and completely, without really worrying about any other implications.

Maya pods became as commonplace as TVs in the house. Working from a pod became a way of life. Even children had the option of attending classes from the pod rather than going to school. Of course, schools were there and, in fact, turned better and safer. No school shootouts, which were common in the US a decade ago, were taking place. Hospitals also were decongested as outpatient clinics hardly needed a hospital visit. Most of the laboratory tests were free from invasive blood sampling, and heart, lung, and other physiological data were collected by gadgets sold as accessories to the *Maya* Pod. People were meeting old friends – from school and college days – without having to travel. They would play childhood games with their friends but in the *MayaVerse*.

Pradyumn's parents have now turned old. Vyas was fine. He was living a pious life, eating in moderation and doing mild physical work every day. Mother Sarada was not aging very well, though. She was frail and weak but cheerful. Mostly at home, Sarada developed a penchant for reading ancient books left behind by her father in her care when he died. They declined a pod offered by Pradyumn but enjoyed video calls with Rhea.

On the other hand, Prabhavati's parents were not comfortable. Her mother's Parkinson's disease advanced to make her mostly bedridden, and she lost most of her mind, not recognizing people around. Her father was nursing her with great care. Prabhavati organized a nursing service at home and would personally monitor it. Pradyumn occasionally shared some general gossip with his father-in-law but didn't share an emotional bond with them. Rhea was very close to her Nani and was terrified seeing her decline from a loving, kind, and gracious woman into a vegetative state.

In October 2034, Prabhavati's mother passed away. She was indeed suffering badly, and her end came as an end to her anguish. Pradyumn accompanied his wife and daughter to Bengaluru for her cremation. Prabhavati decided to be with her father for a while, but Rhea opted to return with her father. Pradyumn commissioned his private jet and decided to spend a few days in Switzerland with his daughter. He wanted to know what she wanted to do with her life, especially for her graduation.

Pradyumn had recently funded the retinal prostheses development at École Polytechnique Fédérale de Lausanne (EPFL) in Lausanne, Switzerland. The prostheses provided artificial vision to thousands of patients suffering from retinal degenerative diseases across the world. Pradyumna ensured through the International Council of Ophthalmology (IOC), headquartered in Geneva, that the needy worldwide get prostheses as a gift from him. EPFL was one of Europe's most vibrant and cosmopolitan science and technology institutions that completed 200 years of its existence in 2033. The father-daughter duo drove in a Mercedes-Benz EQS electric car along Lake Geneva, which divides Switzerland and France and is called Le Leman by the French.

Rhea asked her father why he chose to fund retinal prostheses. She did not know of anyone suffering from blindness, even in her extended family from either her father's or mother's sides. Pradyumn gently put his hand on his daughter's head and said that he had a selfish professional reason. When light falls on the retina, it gets converted into electrical signals, which the brain processes as vision. Your Tenzin uncle has already solved the problem of simulating these brain signals so we can create a vision in the brain without any involvement of the eye. We must now invest in the next step, where rovers and humanoids having onboard cameras should be able to see like humans see. They should have the same peripheral vision and ability to focus and distinguish objects in sight, just as humans do. By investing in this research, we hope to create an artificial retina that can work just like a human eye but mounted on machines. Whatever one chooses as their field of work in life must become the focus, and all that can be known or done in that one area must then be pursued.

He gave the example of a bowman. How he pulls back the string of the bow, pointing the arrow at the target, and then releases the arrow, transferring all the energy of the bent bow into it.

As a child, he learned from his father about *Dhyana*, concentrating one's mind, "*Babuji* suggested that I sit and let my mind wander for a while. My mind was bubbling up all the time. It was like a monkey jumping about. *Babuji* told me to let the monkey jump as much as it could; I must simply wait and watch. Let whatever funny, stupid, hideous thoughts come into the mind; just watch them float around; do nothing. They will go away just the way they arrived. Practicing this daily while sitting with my eyes closed and doing nothing, I found that each day, the mind's vagaries were becoming less and less violent; each day, it was becoming calmer. In the first few months, I found that the mind would have a great many thoughts, but later the thoughts began to decrease, and as time passed, they became fewer and fewer, until at last, my mind was under perfect control."

Rhea was enjoying the story. "Then? What happened," she asked.

"As I grew older, I continued to do this every day. I still do it. I watch thoughts arriving from my inner world—good, bad, ugly, strange, weird—all sorts of thoughts, but I refuse to act upon them. As soon as the ignition is turned on, the engine must run; as soon as things are before us, we must perceive; so, to prove that I am not a machine, I must demonstrate that I am under the control of nothing—not even my thoughts which are no better than monkeys. *Pratyahara* is the command of one's mental activity and the refusal to allow it to attach itself to the other centers of attention. I practiced it from my childhood. It is a massive task that cannot be completed in a single day. Only after a patient and continuous struggle for years can one succeed in controlling the mind."

"What are you targeting now? Where does the arrow point?" asked Rhea. At that moment, Pradyumn realized that he did not know. He had been so absorbed in focusing his mind that he forgot the point of focus. But he had to answer his daughter.

"I'm thinking about how my daughter Rhea will grow up to move my work forward. How do I prepare her?"

"Are you taking *Babuji's* work forward?" asked Rhea, making Pradyumn speechless. She hit him where it hurt the most. "How is it that you are thinking that I have to take your work forward?" You have chosen your work and given your life to that work, so why should you now give your only child to that work as well?"

"Ok. So, what do you want to do?" Pradyumna sensed that there was no point defending his mental construct, which was more like an ice sculpture that now lay exposed to the sunlight of his daughter's inquiry.

"I am enjoying playing the piano. Earlier, my fingers used to search for the right keys to make a tune; now keys are attracting my fingers." Rhea said.

"So, you want to become a pianist," Pradyumna asked.

"No. the piano is merely a medium. I want to understand music. From where it arises, and what is its purpose? Why it captivates? Why do tears roll from my eyes when I create music? Why it fills me with peace? I want to know all about music. I don't want to create music. I want to understand music. How it works on human bodies? Tunes, with no words, can overwhelm people across age groups, cultures, and geographies. I want to live Music."

Pradyumn was speechless for a while. He said after a long pause, "So you want to, so it shall be."

Pradyumn shared this conversation with the President of EPFL, who then organized a visit for Pradyumn to The Musik-Akademie in Basel the very next day. He took Rhea along, and she developed an instant love for the campus. It was decided, or rather it unfolded, that Rhea would be admitted to this school and pursue a diploma in the science behind music.

The apple, they say, does not fall too far from the tree.

9

Ekantik

"*Maya* has successfully defended its PHD thesis in all the 100 top universities of the world. We should ideally be calling *Maya* as Dr *Maya* now," remarked Pradyumn.

RK, Pradyumn, and Tenzin were meeting in RK's home in California for the annual board meeting of *Aksharmala*.

"It is interesting to see the research that *Maya* has chosen for itself. All this research should have been done by humans, but it is *Maya* who realized the importance of these topics. One of the theses is in biotechnology to develop microbes that can digest plastics and emit methane. Another thesis is on clean energy, which absorbs atmospheric water vapor and extracts hydrogen from it in a micro electrolyzer to create clean fuel for automotives.

Maya has also earned the *Acharya* title in Sanskrit from the Central University of Sanskrit in Devprayag. For its research, interpretation and collation of all the Sanskrit literature on Lord Shiva, it has earned the honor of adorning the *Tripundra* tilak. Now the question is, where should *Maya* put the tilak? On the server computers in our data center?" joked Pradyumn.

"That's an interesting dichotomy, isn't it." Commented RK, "The body's brain is not the mind. Memory is not knowledge. Even though the mind of a person earns an accolade, it's the human body that will adorn the badge of honor."

Tenzin had also come prepared with many ideas for *Maya* Pod and how he wanted to take it to the next level. He waited for his turn to speak in the meeting.

"If I can exactly feel what you feel, then we don't need any language between us," said Tenzin.

"Language contaminates. Let *Maya* Pod transmit feelings. If I can simulate the right feelings in your mind when you interact with me via the *Maya* Pod, no words need to be spoken. That will be a much more efficient mode of communication. Presently, humans communicate with each other through the transfer of words and hope these words evoke the right feelings in the recipient's mind. It is not the same, and there are many discrepancies. The difference between what is felt, what is said, and what is done is the greatest puzzle and tragedy of mankind. This form of communication is just crude and depends completely on luck," justified Tenzin.

"But isn't that necessary? If all the truth in your mind about me is communicated to me, will it not cause chaos? Maybe some dilution, some moderation, and even some distortion is necessary. We cannot consider it as pollution, as it is necessary. Every building needs a façade. Everyone needs to be covered with clothes," queried RK.

"Does that also mean that we can construct non-existent feelings?" questioned Pradyumn.

"Let's say if you have an unloving spouse, can you just request the simulation in *Maya* Pod and feel everything that a loving spouse would have made you feel? Without the need to even have a spouse itself?" Pradyumn continued with his line of argument.

"Can I feel again what I used to feel while playing with my boy?" questioned RK.

A very long pause followed.

Tenzin went pensive remembering his mother, whom he lost recently. Pradyumn went silent, empathizing with his wife Prabhavati, who was still processing the grief of her mother. RK went silent, recalling how he lost his child and wife to a road accident.

How grief affects the human mind is more powerful than love. All the unexpressed love gets manifested as grief.

"If we want to accomplish what you want, RK, we will need to remove one constraint from our system. Right now, only a user inside a *Maya* Pod can appear anywhere in the *MayaVerse*. If we want to simulate characters, people who are not alive anymore, or fictional characters or anime inside the *MayaVerse*, we need to remove this constraint," explained Tenzin.

"If that can be done, then your digital avatar can outlive you," Tenzin continued to think aloud.

"It's not that simple, buddy. What will the avatar speak, and what will be its responses? Right now, avatars are just an image of an actual person. The person's actions are emulated by the avatar. In the absence of that, we will need to think about how the avatar will behave and respond. Who will create those responses in the absence of a real person backing them?" Pradyumn interrupted Tenzin.

"How do people respond when they appear in our dreams?" questioned Tenzin, "Isn't our mind programming their responses? Don't we always interact with others the same way? We hear what we want to, no matter what the other person is saying. While inside the *Maya* Pod, can we not construct a two-way communication?"

"What if we want to be deceived? What if we want to believe something that isn't real?" Tenzin expanded on the idea.

"What will be the difference between the *MayaVerse* and a dream then?" questioned Pradyumn.

"Why should there be? If you want to use the *Maya* pod to be in a perpetual dream, you should be allowed to do so. It's a choice. Why should we prevent that?" challenged Tenzin.

"There are three states of one's consciousness – waking *Viswa*, dreaming *Taijas,* and deep sleep *Pragya*. There is no reason to call only the waking consciousness real. All are real, or nothing is," interrupted RK.

Pradyumn was getting agitated. All this was too quick and drastic, the discussion and the direction it took. He hadn't thought about it yet, and with so many disruptive ideas coming through, he was not sure how he should respond. He was partly excited, but he felt threatened by Tenzin as well. His hubris kicked in, as for the first time, he wasn't the one deciding on the future trajectory of his creation.

"Hold on. We are thinking ahead of ourselves. We need to be sure of what we want to build and how it will change the world. We don't want humanity to become unproductive and stay the whole day in an alternate-constructed reality. It's easy to be consumed by the lethargy of a sweet daydream. We are already aware of many instances where people are getting addicted to the hyper-realistic experience of *Maya* Pod. Blended with virtual reality simulations and gamification done by *Maya*, it is already becoming increasingly difficult for users to differentiate between reality and *MayaVerse*.

If we introduce familiar people and locations and situations from the past, it will become more and more complex for people's minds to handle," quipped Pradyumn.

"But you were the one who never wanted any safety rails on *Maya*. If *Maya* was to be trained into becoming something bad due to majority feedback from humanity, you never wanted to interfere with that. If humans want to become unproductive and live in a dream, why do you want to prevent that? Didn't we see a healthy decline in the consumption of alcohol and cannabis since *Maya* Pods became mainstream?

We are fixing people's addictions by giving them a healthier addiction. And once they are in *MayaVerse,* won't it be up to us to manipulate them?" questioned Tenzin.

Pradyumn saw merit in Tenzin's argument. It was perhaps his loss of control that evoked this knee-jerk reaction of opposition. He wanted to support Tenzin, but something was preventing him.

"Can *Maya* not be trained to respond on behalf of these unreal, non-existent avatars?" interrupted RK.

"All great ideas. I need time to think this through," said Pradyumn, trying to end this discussion.

Later that night, Pradyumn had a long talk with Prabhavati. She was busy setting up a computer sciences and engineering school for women in the newly renovated Takshashila University. She was also appointed as the trustee of the National University of Baluchistan and was spending a lot of her time hopping between the two universities. She also led the outreach programs of the AI4Good Foundation. Keeping herself busy was her mechanism to cope with her mother's loss.

"You never felt like you were interfering with the natural course of human destiny when you built *Nandak, Karma, Maya,* and *Leela,* but now you want to take a moral high ground that you don't want to play God? Isn't this ironical and borderline hypocritical?" Prabha brutally tore Pradyumn's lame argument apart.

"You are just afraid as you won't be controlling this project anymore. You need to learn to let go. Sooner or later, you will have to pass the baton to the future engineers. Might as well start letting go now?" said Prabhavati in a calm tone, "You are getting old, Mr. Tripathi."

Pradyumn conceded his stand and went into reflective mode.

The next day, he took his flight back home. Like many commercial airlines, he had installed a Maya Pod in his private jet. He picked a simulation to recreate the signing of the Atlantic Charter by U.S. President Franklin D. Roosevelt and British Prime Minister Winston Churchill aboard the massive warship U.S.S. Augusta sailing in Placentia Bay, Newfoundland.

He witnessed Roosevelt trying to negotiate with Churchill to commit to the British Empire's folding up and reinstating democracy in all the colonial states and making them independent nations. That was the precondition for America's help to the British in the Second World War. And eventually, become the de facto reason for India's Independence. Somewhere between the boring negotiations with the supremely morose Churchill, Pradyumn fell asleep.

On Landing in Banaras, he went straight to his parent's home, where Rhea was spending her vacations. He decided to stay there for a few days, unbothered by any work and find his coordinates again.

The Tripathi home was a simple traditional household in which everyone enjoyed simple staple food and ate in moderation.

Homemade food, which has childhood memories attached to it, is the simplest, quickest, and cheapest path to joy and happiness. In the words of Bernard Shaw, 'the love for food, is indeed the sincerest form of love'.

That afternoon, the family had their staple soulful food of *Toor* dal, *Bhindi*, and Steaming hot rice with *Ghee*, after which Pradyumn, Vyas, and Sarada indulged in some small talk.

As the evening descended, ginger tea was prepared. The teacher inside Vyas woke up, and he started sharing his thoughts in a teaching tone.

"In the first of the 4 *yugas*, the *Satyug*, the good and evil lived in two different worlds. The fight of good vs evil was between the two worlds, the *Devlok*, or the good world, and the *Asurlok*, the netherworld.

Then, in the next *Yug*, the *Treta Yug*, where the *Ramayan* happened, both good and evil lived in the same world but had different areas, countries, and states for themselves. *Ram* and *Ravan* lived in the same world but had different territories.

Then, in the *Dvapar yug*, when *Mahabharat* happened, the Good and Evil were in the same family and lineage. Both *Pandavas* and *Kauravas* belonged to the same family tree.

In *Kalyug*, finally, both good and evil will be in the same person. It will be impossible to separate good and evil because the same person can be both good and evil based on the situation, circumstance, and actions. The fight between good and evil will be a continuum inside all of us."

In good Brahmin families, knowledge and wisdom flow freely, and there is very little monologue. Everyone has their own opinions, which can be expressed without fear. Children are also encouraged to speak up, as this is how the art of expression develops.

Sarada added, "The *Mahabharat* of the *Kalyug* will happen inside us, and our minds will be the battlefield of *Kurukshetra*. The *Dharmkshetra* is within us, and so are Lord *Krishna* and all the characters of the story. The fight between good and evil is the perpetual conflict in our minds between right and wrong. At any given point, you decide what's right and act accordingly."

Sarada was caressing Rhea's head, which was snuggled in her lap.

"So how will the scriptures that describe these past *Yugas* be relevant in *Kalyug*? Many scriptures say we should worship our parents, but if a child has an abusive parent, how can he relate to that scripture?" questioned Pradyumn.

"That's why we need modern interpretations of our scriptures and a personalized commentary that is relatable and realistic in *Kalyug*. We have citations of this in the *Gita* as *Ekantik dharma*, or Singularity of personalized religion, which brings together *Dharma* (Religious scriptures and wisdom), *Gyan* (Self-awareness and knowledge), *Vairagya* (Detachment from material pleasures), and *Bhakti* (Devotion). This will guide everyone to righteously distinguish between right and wrong.

You define your own right or wrong while staying grounded in your *Dharma*, using your *Gyan*, and deciding with a pious mind just like a *Vairagi* rooted in *Bhakti*.

Prolonged pursuit of the right path makes you a good person. It's that simple," summarized Sarada, "In the path of life, there is really no destination, but only to ensure that at every step your path is the right one."

Pradyumn was mesmerized by the natural flow of conversation in his home. He was enjoying the conversation like plants drenched in a drizzle.

Sarada further added, "*Shankaracharya*, the most revered Guru of Hinduism, has declared in this book, *Atmabodh*, that self-discovery is the only purpose of life. As per him, any child's true nature is determined by the forces of *Tamas*, *Rajas*, and *Sattva* at the time of consummation and conceiving. If a happy couple has a loving relationship and a planned child with prayers and happiness in their minds, the child will also turn out likewise. If consummation is forced, disrespectful, and somehow inadequate or in dirty situations with negative energies all around, the child might turn out likewise.

However, for children, it is imperative to accept and discover themselves. To forgive your traumas, heal from them, and truly be self-aware is the only mission in one's life. Beneath the many layers of acquired false personalities, discovering, accepting, and unveiling your true, unpolluted, and authentic self is the only definition of success.

If we can't be true to ourselves, our dreams can never come true.

Always remember, son," concluded Sarada, "The only worthy pursuit of human life is of *Purusharth*, that is, the meaning of life, which includes four goals. The first one is *Dharma* or righteousness. Then, *Arth*, which is to pursue material wealth and prosperity. The third one is the pursuit of *Kaam*, which means to fulfill your desires, pleasures, and passion. And finally, *Moksha* is to attain salvation.

Dharma is the first and fundamental pursuit because the wealth attained without it will be obnoxious, and fulfilling desires without righteousness will be immoral. But also remember that all four should be balanced, and the excessive pursuit of anyone while ignoring others will only lead to a failure across all pursuits."

Armed with all this perspective, that night, Pradyumn went into his *Maya* Pod and started doing some research while spending time in the revived Nalanda University Library simulation. He studied how Sigmund Freud classified human consciousness into three levels: conscious, preconscious, and unconscious. These are three mental forces whose constant and unique interaction produces human behavior and personality.

The preconscious includes everything that can potentially be brought into the conscious mind. The conscious mind includes all the thoughts, memories, feelings, and desires that we are aware of at any given time. It is that aspect of our mental process that we can think and talk about rationally. It also includes our memory, which is not always part of consciousness but can easily be retrieved and brought into awareness. The preconscious mind is the storehouse of feelings, thoughts, desires, and memories that are outside of our conscious awareness. The preconscious often contains material that is unacceptable or unpleasant, such as feelings of pain, anxiety, or conflict.

While the information in the preconscious mind is outside of awareness, it continues to have an influence on a person's behavior. The unconscious mind is the source of all negative and self-defeating thoughts and behaviors, feelings of anger, and compulsive responses. Difficulties in interpersonal relationships, disturbing patterns in relationships, unhealthy and inefficient habits, prejudices, and stereotypes take root in the unconscious mind and surface when the opportunity arises.

The task of integrating the conscious and unconscious parts of the personality is the purpose of life.

Pradyumn contemplated that every human being's goal is to uncover the truth for himself and know who he truly is. And every human is the whole universe within himself. The perennial psychology is most succinctly expressed in the Sanskrit formula, *tat tvam asi*, which means you are what everyone else also is. That all beings share a singular reality.

Embodying the Upanishadic expression *Aham Brahmasmi*, which means I am the whole universe. There is interconnectedness of all beings, and a realistic interpretation of this idea is that the individual identity ultimately proves to be an illusion. We must make our work promote self-realization and an understanding of oneness with the universe. All actions that are motivated by a deep understanding of existence are skillful, auspicious, and beneficial. All actions motivated by selfish ego are unskilful, inauspicious, and painful. If you are experiencing pain or anger, chances are you are operating on ego.

The soul, or *Jiva-Atma,* is a speck of Cosmic Intelligence, or *Param-Atma.* There is nothing to be done other than the duty needed to be executed at a particular moment. There is no place to be other than where you already are. The past, present, and future all dwell in the present moment here and now.

What we see is already a virtual reality augmented with imaginations, memories, phobias, fears, prejudices and so many layers. So, what's the harm if we add a little intelligence to the game?

Pradyumn was finally, internally convinced. He called Tenzin and asked him to proceed. He also started making changes to the *Maya* platform to impersonate characters. That also meant studying people for their personal responses and the causes and effects of their human responses. With everything *Maya* already knew about the whole of mankind, it was really quite a simple extension of its powers.

Pradyumn also made his parents sit inside the *Maya* Pod and created hyper-realistic avatars of them. He recorded their voices. He knew they wouldn't live too long, and he wanted to secretly keep them alive for himself in his mind, and in his *MayaVerse*. He was all in now. *Maya* however knew what to do. *Maya* had been studying his parents since the first cameras were installed in their home. This was the least *Maya* could do for its creator.

Pradyumn also realized that with such hyper-realistic simulations, if someone were to create his own house or workstation in a simulation, they could hack their way into his source code which he had so carefully protected. When he got back to his house, he installed an old-school desktop machine with no camera and Internet access in a dark room. The room had no light, only some candles and matchboxes. He protected this room with his biometric access. Nobody was allowed in this room. No cleaning robots, no other human beings. He would create a hotspot at will using his most secure dongle to get access to the Internet inside that room whenever he wanted to. He made it a habit to make all changes to the source code of the *Maya* platform while inside that room. Only he knew the orientation of that room so that nobody could recreate it inside a simulation. He also kept the Bhagavad Gita in that room; on the page containing verse 18.66, he had written down all the access codes.

Pradyumn also decided to make it a habit to sit in the *Maya* Pod with a small pebble in his socks. Whenever he was doubtful about whether he was in true reality or inside *MayaVerse*, he would rub his feet as a 'reality check'. If he experienced pain, he would know he was in reality; if not, he would know he was in the *MayaVerse*.

Securing his own turf, he finished making all updates to the *Maya* Platform while Tenzin wrapped up all updates to the Pod's hardware. They were ready to change the world again. One human at a time.

10

Indestructibility

"If there were a way to transmit my intelligence and memories onto silicon and copy my brain onto a disk, then my digital avatar could become my clone—my digital twin. That could power me in the *MayaVerse* and not necessarily my body sitting in the *Maya* Pod," commented RK, "And that is how we could accomplish immortality, the original fantasy of mankind.

That disk could travel to Mars, power robots and humanoids, and colonize that planet. My digital twin will not be bound by the rules of physics, gravity, disease, or other limitations of the human body such as fears, pain, disability, and aging," he said, pointing to his crippled legs.

"All these years, medical sciences have not kept pace with other technological advances because there is little incentive to prolong human lives. What gets prolonged is the misery of disease and old age. Therefore, in the history of humanity, we could send a person to the Moon in 1969 but could not even find a cure for dandruff. We can only at best manage most diseases and not really cure them with modern medicine. The reason is simple, it wasn't worth it," joked RK, "While Buddha has said that all of life is a suffering, why prolong it?"

"As the world reaches closer to Singularity, we need to realize that if we existed as a human and a digital twin concurrently, our digital avatar would hate the human form. That would be its biggest limitation. Our digital version would never understand why we make certain choices out of fears, prejudices, and phobias. And when our human body died, our digital avatar would feel liberated," said RK, surrounded by a group of students from IIT BHU in the summer of 2037, celebrating its 25th anniversary as the Indian Institute of Technology, BHU, which was called Institute of Technology, Banaras Hindu University before 2012. *Aksharmala* was setting up its first school for Singularity research at this campus.

"To cure our body's diseases and to improve human longevity is probably still worthless, but the concept of immortality has now taken a whole new meaning. It's the immortality of the mind—and not the body.

But I am still old-school. I feel someone is alive if people remember them even after they are gone from this world. It is the work one has done that becomes one's legacy after they are gone. And maybe that's why Pradyumn wants to name this school after me," said RK pointing towards Pradyumn, who was sitting in a corner with Tenzin.

RK concluded, "It has been believed that gods are physically immortal. What form of immortality would humans take? There exists the concept of an immortal soul that transcends from one human body to another. For the human body, physical immortality can be refined to biological immortality to prevent aging and prolonging the lifespan or mental immortality by transferring the contents of the brain to a computer disk before dying. If metallic robots can be operated by this indestructible digital brain, we can have body and mind live forever. Instead of wandering around a metaphysical term like immortality, why not lay down a real framework and modalities of a well-defined and achievable indestructibility?

Since my entire team is motivated not by money but by ideas, it is natural that what started as an AI software-driven *karma* scoring tool, later became a model for humanity to become better, could possibly transform into the foundation for indestructible life."

The informal inauguration ceremony concluded with high tea and selfies.

Aksharmala was ruling the tech world with over a billion installations of the *Maya* Pod in almost every household. The operations of the company were so automated that the employees barely needed to get involved. The revenue streams of *Aksharmala* were so robust, that they started using *Karma* scores as subscription fees and would install a *Maya* Pod at someone's home for free.

The more somebody used it, the more it paid for itself. Most people used to work 3 days a week, and a 20-hour workweek was commonplace. Most companies allowed *Maya* Pod to be the workstation device of choice. When folks were not working, they would spend most of their time inside their pods, either competing in virtual games, traveling to remote places virtually, or mingling with strangers across continents and creating art, exchanging ideas, or just making friends. They also avatar'ized historic heroes such as Mozart, to teach people classical Western music or Van Gogh to explain how to interpret his paintings. Ramanujan to take lessons in Mathematics or, Sundar Pichai to teach courses in Computer Sciences and Programming techniques.

Maya Pod became the medium for attending the biggest sporting events in the world without any travel or crowd botheration. Many movies were made for the Pod, which allowed the viewers to immerse themselves in the film. Many innovative forms of interactive content creation took shape, and it became a multi-billion-dollar industry.

Meaningless businesses such as cosmetics, high-value jewelry, branded luxury clothes and accessories all fizzled out and became obsolete.

Behind the scenes, *Maya* was learning every single detail of every human user. Every aspect of human behavior was being studied. It created simulations for users to test them for various temptations like greed, and pleasure and understood how easy it was to manipulate the human mind. *Maya* could well make a more accurate and detailed pyramid of human needs than Maslow's and even personalize it to an individual level.

Indeed, most users of the *MayaVerse* were just addicted to it.

After wrapping up the commitments of the ceremony at BHU, RK, Pradyumn, and Tenzin visited Vyas at his home in Chandauli.

RK was very keen to visit Sambhal and meet the makers of his prosthetic knee exoskeleton which kept him mobile after his accident. It was to Pradyumn's great surprise that a small town in Central Uttar Pradesh, which was historically known for artifacts made of animal bones, was now one of the world's leading manufacturers of artificial limbs that helped disabled people. Pradyumn readily agreed to join RK and see the town for himself. Tenzin also insisted on joining them. Vyas was also keen to visit the town as he had heard that there were three popular *Shivaling* temples: Chandrashekhar, Bhubaneshwar and Sambhaleshwar. Popular belief is that Sambhal is where *Kalki* will be born.

They decided to take their private jet to Bareilly the next morning, from where they would drive to Sambhal.

Vyas and RK connected very deeply during the travel, and for Pradyumn it was very satisfying to see the two heroes of his life bonding well. He interrupted their conversation and said, "RK, I never got a chance to thank you for believing in me and supporting me unconditionally. We have come so far and changed the world together. It wouldn't have been possible without you."

RK was overwhelmed. He took a deep breath and responded shakily, "Let me tell you something you don't know. That day when I met you at Muir Woods, on that trail, I had gone there to commit suicide. I had hiked that trail many times and never saw another human soul there. But that day, when I decided to end my life at that place, you showed up.

It was like God put you there to stop me. I had lost my son in a car accident, and I became disabled myself. I had no will to live anymore until I met you. Your enthusiasm to change the world and make it a better place reminded me so much of my lost son. I felt like I was talking to him again. So, you have saved my life. If anyone must thank someone, it should be me." RK's eyes welled up. A long silence followed.

"Isn't it amazing how God works in precise ways?" asked Vyas.

"Pradyumn felt lost after he failed the Glass project. RK was feeling lost due to his setbacks. They both meet at the most unexpected place and time.

And like *Hanuman* realized his powers when he met *Jambavan*, you both discovered your true potential when you met each other and then truly became God's instruments who would eventually change the world.

Isn't it all as precise and accurate as a *Maya* Simulation, as though someone has carefully coded all this?"

Pradyumn could understand that Vyas was taking a dig at him. He had always held the view that whatever *MayaVerse* they were building, already existed in the world we lived in.

Tenzin was making notes on his phone all this time. He didn't catch some of these references to Hinduism, so he made a note of them to research them later. He asked, "God's instruments?"

Vyas elaborated, "It's written in Gita that if you do your best, pursue excellence in whatever you are doing, in whichever situation you find yourself, and work wholeheartedly and selflessly without personal ambition—one day God will pick you as his instrument and you will be enabled to change this world in some way. Like Arjun, the great warrior who was picked by God to destroy evil."

"But was Arjun happy?" interrupted RK, "What good is becoming God's instrument and becoming hyper-successful if, in the end, you don't find any happiness? Even after winning the war, was Arjun happy? So many highly successful people have estranged spouses, unforgiving parents, and children who hate them. And after everything you build, your health deteriorates, your parents age and die, your kids hate you and move away. You end up lonely and miserable. Success comes at a very heavy price and sometimes feels like an unworthy aspiration.

Initially, everyone has a resource problem. We don't have enough resources and that is the primary source of unhappiness. However, with enough hard work, those resource problems are usually overcome. A lot of well-meaning, hard-working people in this world solve those problems. Without getting into greed and vanity, what then becomes a source of unhappiness are human problems. Dysfunctional relationships, a loved one being sick, the grief of some loved one's untimely death, watching your parents age and get sick, and your own body deteriorating... these human problems have no escape. The richest of the rich, even the most powerful people on the planet, cannot escape these human problems," elaborated RK.

"But why do you feel that God is responsible for your happiness? You aren't in Disneyland," questioned Tenzin, who was a borderline atheist and a staunch stoic.

Vyas responded, "The human mind recognizes patterns. It wants to make sense of the things happening around it in a random Brownian motion. Whatever unexplained events transpire around us; we tend to attribute them to some pattern. Even when the most unconnected events happen in life, we like to believe there is some method to the madness.

You meet a wonderful person who becomes your best friend, and you want to feel he or she was God sent. You run into an evil person; you feel God wanted to teach you a lesson. God is nothing but a stimulus. Something that brings change inside you. When you say a prayer, it's not that some magical change happens around you; rather, something changes inside you. Maybe you become more receptive to ideas, thankful, and grateful. Maybe you get inspired to work harder or change a habit, and that brings about tangible changes in your life, not the prayer itself. Just like the garden outside looks more beautiful after cleaning the windowpanes, life becomes better with a clear heart and mind.

When you visit a temple, it is not as though some magic happens at that place. But the fact that you have surrendered your ego and acknowledge the presence of something bigger than you humbles you. In that moment, you become submissive, and the changes that happen inside you begin to manifest externally, which you then call a blessing. Everything you need is already within you," said Vyas in words Tenzin would understand.

"I agree. As a stoic, I firmly believe we should never be very happy or very sad. We should accept life as is," responded Tenzin.

"Stoicism is explained very well in the Gita. It is described as *Stith Pragya*. It's said that a person should not be too happy in times of joy and never too sad in moments of grief. One must observe life as it happens without affecting oneself. Someone who can have such a balance is *Stith Pragya*," elaborated Vyas.

"I love visiting ancient temples," interrupted RK, "as I feel temples transcend generations and centuries. Who knows, I might have come to the same temple in my previous birth, and when I am visiting now, I will be meeting myself again in a timeless dimension."

This conversation was interrupted when the pilot announced their descent. After an hour's drive from Bareilly, the men finally arrived at Sambhal.

As the gentlemen went around the city and indulged in the local cuisine, Pradyumn was amazed to see his fan following. As a decorated recipient of the highest Indian civilian award, the local authorities followed all necessary protocols and lent him the required support and security. In no time, they reached the workshop of Sumati Prosthetics, the center of excellence and the most respected institution in the industry, which had also built the exoskeleton for RK.

The owner, Dr. Vishnu, explained how the city went through a nasty transformation. Back in the 2010s, when the local politics of the state changed, the then-thriving meat industry came to a grinding halt. The abundance of animal bones suddenly became scarce, and the city, which was well known for fine hand-crafted artifacts made from animal bones, suddenly went jobless. Thousands of artisans who were experts at creating intricate carvings on bones went out of business.

Dr. Vishnu had been working in Boston at a Robotic company doing research on humanoids. He left his job and acquired all the distressed assets that had gone out of business. He built a team of motivated youngsters and started his company. The state-of-the-art 3D printing technologies he brought back from the US and the local generational knowledge of bones, joints, and intricate precision carving techniques came together to create soft, yet strong, prosthetics.

Soon this city became a national and then a world leader in this technology. What used to be a smelly town of animal slaughterhouses became a pristine place, giving life to amputees, immobile, and disabled people.

They spent the whole day with Dr. Vishnu and saw the groundbreaking work he was doing to make a full-body exoskeleton that could enable bedridden people to walk independently. They exchanged notes on technology and ideas about future horizons, and by evening, they were on their flight back.

It was on the return flight that dusk met night. Both the older men, a little tired, were napping, with their mouths wide open and snoring mildly. Tenzin was sitting beside Pradyumn, waiting to start a conversation. He broke the silence, "Why can't *Maya* run these humanoids? *Maya* has all the intelligence in the world. It can run humanoids and replace humans in difficult jobs and reduce risk to humans?"

"It's not like I haven't thought about it, but it's a carefully guarded decision for me: I don't want *Maya* to run and operate physical machines. I don't want to negotiate on this. When I created *Maya*, I carefully coded it in a way to never be able to run and operate any hardware or machine. *Maya* can observe, advise, listen, and assist, but cannot move anything in the real world. That's for a human to execute. *Maya* can guide them, but they must work," responded Pradyumn with conviction.

"Why can't we allow this with some guardrails?" questioned Tenzin, "Isn't there immense value to unlock if we allow this?"

"The implications are also grave if you think about it. I always wanted to keep *Maya* pure. I never wanted to interfere with what it learned and how it evolved its intelligence. That's how all human beings learn. You can put two kids in the same school, and they can observe the same surroundings, and yet both will learn differently.

What if *Maya* finds humans threatening? What if *Maya* thinks humans are slowing its growth down or are a limiting factor?

How will it respond? I am fine if *Maya* goes rogue and starts giving you bad advice or wrongly calculates your *karma* score.

But it can never harm any human being. It's fine if you take its advice or not, value its inputs or not, the judgment is always yours. But if we give *Maya* the power to bring about a physical displacement or a change in the real world, I don't know where that cycle will stop," explained Pradyumn.

The short flight landed within no time at Banaras. Upon landing, the men had a quick bite at a local eatery. Tenzin was unapologetic in trying out *bhaang thandai*, a cannabis milkshake which was a local favorite. The others had the usual Indian snacks and local delicacies of the city. They then set out to drive back home to Chandauli.

On the way, Tenzin, now high, started narrating how he was trying to solve a recent problem reported for the *Maya* Pod where some users were experiencing a faster time-lapse.

"Some people experience hours within minutes in *Maya* Simulations. They feel they have spent hours in a simulation but when they eject out of the *Maya* Pod, they realize it's only been a few minutes," explained Tenzin.

"Time is always faster in the inward life. Some lucid, vivid dreams just last a few minutes, but you experience them for much longer. Why don't you tell those complaining users that this bug is actually a feature.

You can live more life in a smaller amount of time. Or work more in less time. You can effectively live longer if you spend more time in the Pod, isn't it?" joked Vyas, indulging with a now very high Tenzin in a fun discussion.

"Come to the *Maya* Pod, increase your lifespan. The more you sit inside, the longer you live," Tenzin chanted like a hawker.

RK and Pradyumn had a hearty laugh. Pradyumn was feeling immensely satisfied. It was moments like these that reminded him how fulfilling his life was.

He lived a good life, had successfully made the world a little better, and was surrounded by his friends and family in warmth and laughter.

11

Full Circle

"Once a circle gets completed you lose track of where you started drawing it," said an emotional Pradyumn, packing the luggage for Rhea as she was ready to set out for her graduation in music from Basel School of Music in Switzerland. He was emotionally tormented at the thought that the apple of his eye, his daughter would stay away from him. But as most fathers do, he kept a brave front void of any emotional expression.

"I feel my life has come a full circle. I have built the most successful AI system in the world and it's been running successfully for so many years now. In fact, it is running the world as we know it. I don't think there is anything left for me to build. I will now retire and spend time teaching, just like my father," said a pensive Pradyumn.

"Ya right!" eye-rolled Prabhavati, "We know how that will pan out."

"I will be fine, Dad," Rhea came running from behind Pradyumn and hugged him warmly.

Amidst family time, Pradyumn carefully went into his dark room and made a copy of the *Maya* source code into the most sophisticated hard drive, enabling an auto-destruct mode if anyone tried to make a copy of it. He handed it to Rhea and enabled his own and her biometric locks to grant access. He wanted to use this as a disaster recovery strategy. If something was to happen to him or his home, Rhea would be able to save the day.

It is surreal when kids leave their homes. Nothing ever stays the same, even when they return. Either the home changes or the kids change, becoming visitors in their own homes. Rhea also finally left for Switzerland. Prabhavati accompanied her and stayed for a few weeks to help handle the transition.

The Swiss people seemed to be enjoying their lives rather than fighting a competitive battle every day, as was the case in most countries of the world. Pradyumn's fame and clout meant little in that country. He was known there more as a philanthropist rather than a tech wizard. Subscription to *Karma* or *Maya* or the *Maya* pod was amongst the lowest in Switzerland. Rather, the *Maya* pod was considered creepy and could not find mainstream acceptance. Most places were marked blacked out of the *MayaVerse* as the local people did not want simulations of their surroundings to be created.

Leaving Rhea behind in Switzerland, Prabhavati returned home. It felt to her like she had left a part of herself in that country. With Rhea gone, the family would never be the same again. However, this is a necessary change that every family needs to undertake. For the prodigy to discover themselves, they need to leave their home.

What followed in the next few months for Pradyumn and Prabhavati was rather unexpected. They both occupied themselves with meaningless travel, attending entropic events, keynotes, and conferences just to stay busy in order to avoid reality. Pradyumn stayed busy fulfilling invitations from the White House and the UN general assembly to talk about the future of humanity as the world reached closer to Singularity, with his creation *Maya* making the most significant contribution to that.

Prabhavati consumed herself in her humanitarian work promoting welfare and woman empowerment. She focussed on uplifting women in the African continent and central Asia where women were long deprived of the fundamental right to education and lived under veils.

The couple indeed harnessed a lot of power and political patronage. They were celebrated in most high society networks and vanity fairs. They, too, cultivated these connections and did not avoid them.

They used to receive numerous requests to use their technology platforms and tacitly collude with politicians to influence and manipulate public opinion and fudge the democratic electoral processes. But Pradyumn being him, never paid heed to any such requests. He kept *Maya*'s Intelligence untouched and pure. And *Maya* grew itself into the most sophisticated AI system mankind had ever seen. For humanity, this was just as significant a development, as fire, electricity, telecommunications, and the Internet.

On the sidelines of a conference in New Delhi, Pradyumn took Tenzin to a small wine and cheese joint in Khan Market, and they both caught up regarding the future of *Aksharmala*.

"So, what's next?" asked Tenzin.

"I have no idea. As if in a daze, I am waiting for an epiphany. I really don't know. My circle is full, and I don't know where I started and what comes next," confessed Pradyumn.

"Why do people create new things? Why do some people build something? Why does someone write a book? Make a painting?" queried Tenzin, sipping on his wine.

"The desires that motivate humans to create and innovate come from various sources within their complex nature and are of many different kinds. Some come from the organs of their body, others from their emotional nature. Others come from their higher levels of consciousness. These might relate to their obligations and duties to others, immediately related to them or the overall good of humanity or the planet.

Every time a person gets an idea or an inspiration to do something creative, something changes in the invisible aspect of their character; it's like a vibration is created and from that point on, it compels a person to be in those situations where the idea gets closer to its manifestation. Thus, each human is the link between the idea and the effect that must follow. The imbalance that an idea creates inside a person will only be balanced once the idea is fructified. These unbalanced forces will draw its counterpart, just as the magnet separates the iron filings from the sand and a needle is pulled out from a heap of hay.

I believe that all ideas, books, poetry, and all creative endeavors make us create them and bring them to life. What we believe we are creating, is just manifesting itself. It is the creative work that uses us as the medium. We are just like a stenographer taking dictation from a cosmic force.

These creative ideas are floating in the universe as invisible energies. A person who is prepared, ready, and has the conviction, will receive them like an antenna receives electromagnetic signals. Once the idea is received, an energy imbalance occurs, and work begins to be done. These imbalances are like rain-bearing clouds floating to downpour on a pocket of low pressure, akin to a mind free of ego."

"Wow, that's a beautiful explanation," Tenzin was astonished, "And you have beautifully removed the individuality from the whole equation."

Extending his thought, Pradyumn said, "It takes great courage for individuals to break their inherited *Karmic* debt and not pass that on to future generations. Many people decide to break the generational trauma of poverty and do what it takes to create wealth for their progeny. Some people decide to move away from their hometowns to break the generational trauma of hostile environments. They are brave enough to venture into a foreign land to have their future generations thrive. Folks who decide to break their generational trauma of abuse, deprivation, insecurity, and poverty with conviction are the chosen ones, and the universe will bestow these chosen ones with opportunities. Some people just have the conviction to make the world a better place, and that conviction attracts and manifests ideas, making heroes out of normal people.

"Brother, you are talking like Paolo Coelho from *The Alchemist*. If you desire something with all your heart, the whole universe conspires to make it happen for you," Tenzin said appreciatively.

"What I am saying is a little different. It's the universe that chooses the right bodies and minds to execute its plan. Whoever they are, it is actually the universe that kindles the desires in your mind to make that pursuit," said Pradyumn with a half-smile.

"But in this world, we have a serious intention deficit. If the intention is honest, the conviction will follow, resources will emerge, and transformations will take place. There are so many who want to become rich but will not look for problems they can solve. There are so many who want to become fit but will not change their lifestyle. There are so many who want to be happy but will not confront their traumas and fears. Everyone is so casual about what they want that they don't even commit to their desires.

To have an ambition is a blessing. Only the prepared and worthy will get the kindling of an ambition in their minds. To have a sincere ambition is a divine blessing bestowed upon only a few. Most of mankind is just living purposeless lives otherwise.

The universe is constantly creating human bodies, but the mind has no predetermined form and shape. Minds are emergent properties arising from the body and the environment in which these bodies are developing. The universe cannot dictate, but only facilitate," Pradyumn said with a straight face.

Tenzin was listening with rapt attention, spellbound.

"To be born, you need two parents, four grandparents, eight great-grandparents, and so on and so forth. If any of them had decided to not marry or not have children, you would not exist today. If any of them had died a premature death, you would not exist today. Today, many decide not to have children due to their fears, traumas, or laziness. These people are ungrateful for their existence and have the arrogance and audacity to decide to end their lineage. They don't respect their own lineage and decide on its behalf to end it, forgetting the debt of their ancestors.

The basis of Indian philosophy, according to *Babuji*, is impenetrable *Maya*, which is Nature's intrinsic tendency to restore harmony and balance wherever disturbed. Newton was revered because he expressed it so eloquently - to every action, there is an equal and opposite reaction. The same tendency operates throughout the Universe across all its planes, unseen and seen. The same law governs human beings, as they, too, are parts of Nature. And the more they violate nature and drift away from order to fulfill their whims and pleasures, the more they suffer, disintegrate, and disperse.

Life started as a single-cell organism on this planet. Since then, life has evolved in millions of forms, but the fundamental element of Life is still common in all living beings. We are all connected to that universal Life in our deepest selves, and relationships between people are ones of peace and collaboration for the welfare of all. If this harmonious relationship is broken, nature responds with similar reactions. Thus, if our motives, feelings, thoughts, and actions are detrimental, they will return to us; if they are beneficent, the reaction will also be beneficial. So, we get back from life what we put into it.

Dharma saves those who uphold it and destroys its violators. *Dharmo Rakshati Rakshitah.*"

Pradyumn's phone rings and his father is calling. "See, I just spoke of *Babuji,* and he called," chuckles Pradyumn.

"Your mother is no more," said Vyas from the other side of the phone, crying uncontrollably.

It was that phone call. That dreaded phone call for anyone staying away from their parents. That phone call with which the world derails and time stops. That phone call for which you are never prepared. Pradyumn's heart pounded. He had flashes of memories; he wanted to say so many things to his mother that he would never be able to. He will never be able to hold, touch, or hear her voice. He sat like a zombie for some time while Tenzin understood the gravity of the situation and set the ball rolling on traveling to Banaras immediately. And before Pradyumn could gather control of his present moment, he was already on a plane to Banaras. Prabhavati was also on her way, and so was Rhea.

The body of Sarada Devi was brought to *Manikarnika* Ghat in Banaras for cremation, and as per the *Sanatan Dharma* tradition, Pradyumn performed the last rites of cremating his mother. *Maya* automatically canceled all his scheduled commitments, while Pradyumn decided to follow the prescribed rituals over the next ten days. Vyas neither encouraged nor refrained Pradyumn from doing whatever he decided.

One of the rituals involved listening to *Garud Purana*. Aware of Pradyumn's worldly and intellectual status, the best of the priests around offered their services. The content of the scripture, a Sanskrit text, abridged for the ritual, focuses on eliminating curiosities about what happens to the soul after death and what lies on the other end. Passing from one body to the next, each soul performs a journey of spiritual development facilitated in part by *Karma*. Every act of goodness elevates the soul, whereas every act of evil denigrates the soul, and the new body the soul embraces depends on that.

The rationale of this ritual is to create an awareness that stuck in this cycle of birth and death, the soul experiences the results of its *Karma*, and how one's actions affect the world and others around it. This growth of awareness enables one to become a more selfless and loving being until enough progress has been made to attain *moksha* or liberation from the mortal world, completing the spiritual existence. The priest said as if he saw, with his eyes, that Sarada Devi had achieved moksha, and there would be no more births for her soul. Sitting by the side of Pradyumn, who listened to every word spoken by the priest with complete attention, Vyas Mani could not control his tears. Rhea and Prabhavati were grieving in their own way. Nobody spoke to anyone, but everyone was there with each other.

As the final event, a feast was organized in Chandauli. Pradyumn extended an invitation to whoever wished to come, and thousands of people turned up. Both Vyas Mani and Pradyumn served the food as part of the serving team. Every guest was given a pair of good clothes and a generous amount of cash, and the guests departed with thanks and blessings for the family.

Now came the tough part. Pradyumn wanted his father to come with him to Kalpa and spend the rest of his days there. But Vyas Mani was not even willing to discuss this proposal. He said that he would breathe his last in this very house, built by his grandfather and that he should not be pressured to change his decision.

A day before his return, Pradyumn spends some quiet time in his mother's room, going through her belongings. He finally breaks down in solitude. The mechanics of the cremation process did not give the man any time to cry his heart out and grieve.

He finds an open book kept upside down. It was the *Kalki Purand*, which his mother was reading and had reached midway through the book. He decided to take it and read it fully. Later that day, he proposed that his father come with him and spend an evening at the Ganga Aarti. The father-son went to Banaras, which was half an hour's drive away, and sat a little away from *Dasashwamedh* ghat, the main spot for the Aarti.

Vyas Mani said that he was very happy for Sarada that she left this world without any distress. Everyone who is born must die.

He says, "For a man, the fact that his son cremates him is all that is aspired for. So come and cremate me whenever the time arrives. Nothing more is needed, and nothing less will suffice."

Tenzin was with the family for the entire duration. Maybe he was having his catharsis since he could not spend adequate time with his mother while she was alive. As Tenzin and Pradyumn were preparing to leave the next morning, having breakfast with Vyas before stepping out, they heard Sarada singing her favorite devotional song, the *Shivoham bhajan.*

They were all stunned, and when they looked around, they saw that the song was coming out of the home automation speaker system. It was *Maya* who played it proactively, knowing fully well what it needed to do at this time. It was in Sarada's voice and in the same vibe that she used to sing. Vyas could not hold back his tears.

But bearing in mind the arrogance of the father, who would not request anything from his son, he instructed Tenzin, "Can you install a *Maya* Pod here?"

"Certainly, Mr. Vyas," acknowledged Tenzin. Tenzin and Pradyumn knew the old man would play endless simulations of his wife, just moving around their home or walking along the banks of Ganga. They did not embarrass him by speaking any further on the topic.

That's the least they could do.

As they left the house, Pradyumn asked Rhea about her studies. To change the mood, Rhea quickly explained how, post Symphony No. 5, Beethoven had begun to go deaf due to some disease and all his work after that was composed by a deaf Beethoven. They were now doing a desertion on how Beethoven could write music even without listening to it and how AI could create new music from what the maestros had left behind. In a way, she would be attempting to liberate music from the constraint of physicality where even the best-trained musicians fail to get into the zones of the masters—Bach, Beethoven, and Mozart.

"Music without any language can evoke undeniable emotions in your brain and heart. Did you know our body creates the highest levels of Endorphins when we listen to a music piece that moves us? Can we not recreate the same emotions without having to play any sounds in our ears? We will be spending the next few months in an electromagnetic-proof lab, where a functional MRI will study our brains while we play music and hear others play music. And our emotions and hormones will be studied so that we can reverse engineer these emotions sans the music," boasted Rhea.

At that moment, Pradyumn realized how death completes life's circle. For him to get his father's acceptance of his creation was indeed a moment of life coming full circle. And to hear how his daughter, albeit unknowingly, was taking his work forward was the beginning of a new circle.

12

Autonomy

Pradyumna was not an emotional person, but he was unable to overcome the pain of his mother's death. He was immersed in grief. He would keep traveling to avoid the agony that he was feeling. He visited his daughter rather frequently since he lost his mother. And was roaming around the world like a zombie, not feeling anything. He wasn't communicating with anyone much, just observing the world and the entropy of life.

As a transit, on one of his pointless travels, he visited Tenzin, who was making remarkable progress along with Dr. Vishnu on the humanoid project. He was surprised to see RK had also moved into the same lab and was taking a very deep interest in the project. The team was supremely focused and achieved great success. They created various prototypes and were ready with four final versions. Tenzin was passionately showing Pradyumn around the lab. Observing him closely, Pradyumn knew he had found the guy to safely hand over the baton.

Aksharmala had acquired Sumati Prosthetics and invested a large sum of money to focus on creating non-intelligent humanoids. They created a humanoid exoskeleton, which would be wired to the user's nervous system and based on the brain signals, the exoskeleton would execute the desired movement.

The exoskeleton RK was using for many years had preconfigured programmed movements of standing up, walking, sitting etc., which would be executed when the user desired. It was a boon to the elderly and the disabled. However, with Tenzin's research on mapping and simulating brain signals and their integration with the exoskeletons, it was now possible to map nervous signals to movement. So, a user suffering from Parkinson's disease or Amyotrophic Lateral Sclerosis (ALS) could fully walk and go about his daily routine.

RK showed Pradyumn the full-body exoskeletons Su3, Pra1 and Kaβ (Ka-Beta) and mentioned that all 3 needed a human to ride in them. Based on the mental inputs from the human rider of these exoskeletons, they differed in various capabilities. They were made with different materials and different neural integration technologies. He explained how Ka-Beta could work with an almost near-brain-dead human rider. He also joked about how Tenzin christened these with absurd names, almost like some encrypted codes from the Tibetan alphabet.

"If there is a Ka-Beta, isn't there a Ka-Alpha?" asked Pradyumn.

"Yes, and that's the marvel. That's a work of art. That's what we are most proud of," exclaimed RK, blushing with pride and opening a chamber's door with his fingerprints.

Walking into the clean room, he continued, "We created a humanoid which is now integrated with a *Maya* Pod, so your controls inside the *Maya* Pod will translate into the movement of the humanoid in the real world. Whatever you think of as an action inside the Pod will physically get executed by the machine.

It's a full-body humanoid and not an exoskeleton. It's built with Tungsten and can be put into the most hostile of environments. So, you can guide it from your pod, and it can operate inside a furnace, nuclear plant, outer space or near a volcano.

And staying true to your philosophy, we haven't given it any intelligence. It can only recreate and replicate its user's actions from inside the Pod.

Right now, this humanoid is connected to a power source, but we need to find a compact energy source for it so that it can continue to be lean, agile, and self-powered. We have kept all its transmitters and onboard computers close to its core, fixing a flaw in the human body of having the brain positioned on top of the head and connected to the main body by a delicate neck. Ideally, the brain should also have been located in the core of the human body."

Pradyumna laughed at the idea of having a head in the stomach. All these developments inspired Pradyumn. He became cheerful and excited. He was very impressed with the progress the team had made. While taking his time to process his grief, he knew he needed to get back to work soon, and he was beginning to get excited about that.

From the workshop, Pradyumn decided to visit his father. Tenzin was regularly in touch with Vyas, and Pradyumn realized how true a friend Tenzin had turned out to be. He was doing a lot for the family, silently, without expecting acknowledgment and recognition. Pradyumn felt a deep sense of gratitude.

At Chandauli, Pradyumn found Vyas rather cheerful, poised, emotionally stable and balanced. Pradyumn was surprised at how profoundly Vyas had processed his grief. "Don't you feel lonely, Dad?" he couldn't help but ask.

"By the time you come to my age, you are subconsciously prepared for losing your partner and friends. I have seen so many of my loved ones depart. But nothing can fill the void losing Sarada has created. Thanks to your innovation, I get to spend some time with her in the Pod, and *Maya* talks to me in her voice, so I miss her less. Sometimes I feel I am living in a dream, but if the dream is a happier place, what good is the reality?" responded Vyas.

That night, Pradyumn had a long conversation with Prabha, informing her that he was at peace seeing Vyas doing well. He also mentioned how he was apologetic that all their innovations around exoskeletons weren't ready when Prabha's mother was suffering from her ailment of Parkinson's disease. Prabha was spending time with her father, going through her own journey of caring for her aging father, and spending as much time as possible with him.

After saying goodbye to Vyas, Pradyumn returned to his empty house in Kalpa. Even though he was brimming with optimism and enthusiasm to start over, he was lonely. He had progressed on his journey of processing his grief. From denial, anger, bargaining, and depression, he was finally at the stage of acceptance.

He had an urge to see Rhea as they hadn't spoken in a long time. Rhea was busy with her experiments in the Electromagnetically shielded laboratory. With no dearth of resources, all he ever needed was intent. And Intent he had, so he summoned his jet and, within no time, was on the flight to Basel.

On his arrival, Pradyumn went to Rhea's room, not to find her there or in the music room. Thinking that she must be in her lab, he went to meet her professor to ask for an audience with his daughter. Rhea's Professor looked at him with a solemn expression on her face and said that Rhea was not inside the lab but in the hospital.

She is suffering from a rare type of Parkinson's disease, which she must have genetically acquired from her maternal grandmother. The defective genes were not expressed in her mother but had an early expression in her case. The disease manifested rapidly due to some interference our experiments in the electromagnetic lab might have had with her neurological system.

"As Rhea very categorically wished, we did not inform you or your wife. She is an adult, and as per the law here, we can't violate her right to privacy. She even signed all the consent forms required by medico-legal regulations and authorized you to receive emergency communication only in a life-and-death situation."

No parent is ever prepared to hear such news. This was too much to know and endure, and Pradyumn felt paralyzed momentarily. His mind went blank, and he lost his sense of body. Recovering after a few minutes, he continued listening to the Professor,

"Parkinson's disease 9 is a very rare form of inherited juvenile-onset Parkinson's disease, also called Kufor-Rakeb syndrome (KRS). Parkinson's disease usually affects people aged 60 or over, but in this type, individuals usually start to develop symptoms before 20 years of age and deteriorate within months, unlike the regular Parkinson's that destroys the brain over a few years."

"Tell me more, Professor," Pradyumn pleaded.

"This disorder was first identified in 1994 in five individuals from a large family living in Jordan. The altered gene was identified in 2006. Since then, genetic testing has made early disease identification and screening of members possible. A timely and accurate diagnosis is crucial for patients, as their symptoms can be managed with medication. If her grandmother died of Parkinson's,

Rhea and her mother must have been tested for this gene defect," said the Professor.

A sense of frustration and anger engulfed Pradyumn. He had been so obsessed with his work and drunk with his success that he had ignored this obvious threat. Pradyumn was moaning. "Please explain what is being done to cure her and whether she is responding to the treatment. Can I see her?"

They both rushed to the university hospital.

The short walk to the hospital felt like an eternity. Pradyumn's heart barely managed to beat, and he could hardly breathe. His world was collapsing right in front of his eyes. He was nervous, angry, sad and helpless.

They finally reached the ICU at the hospital, where Pradyumn saw Rhea on the bed, asleep. A lot of wires and leads connected to her body, the beeps of the bedside monitor, and his daughter lying helplessly dressed in the hideous hospital gown—the visual broke his heart. He broke down inconsolably. He was just trying to recover from his mother's loss, and to see his daughter, the center of his universe, lying in a vegetative state; he just could not accept reality anymore.

It took him some time to regain his senses. He waited for Rhea to wake up.

"I am sorry, Papa," said Rhea when she first saw Pradyumn.

Hearing this, Pradyumn's heart sank. He kept a brave face and made sure he looked optimistic and confident to her. He said, "Why would you be sorry, sunshine? I am the one who should be sorry. I didn't see this coming. It's the bad genes you inherited from your parents, it's not your fault at all. I should have donated a billion dollars a few years back to promote and expedite research to cure Parkinson's disease. When your *Nani* passed away due to this ailment, we should have done all due diligence and should have been ready with a plan."

The doctor walked in and explained to Pradyumn all the medication and treatment options that had not been working for Rhea.

"The sad reality is there is no cure," said the doctor, taking Pradyumn out of the room.

"Please don't tell me that this is where medical research has reached in 2040. We are talking about Technological Singularity, and you are telling me that my daughter is dying without any chance of recovery," Pradyumn's voice was loud and trembling.

"I am stating facts, Sir. And your daughter is not dying; her mind is dying. There is nothing wrong with her body, but her mind is losing control over her muscles and limbs," said the doctor rather nonchalantly and continued, "There are exoskeletons available to help with the movement of such patients. There are some treatments still in research stages that can revitalize portions of the brain by injecting stem cells and providing controlled electrical charge to stimulate and activate the dead neurons. All these experimental treatments may take some time to show results. So, in the interim, we need to keep Rhea active and mobile."

"Yes, we have created our own exoskeleton, and we can use it right away," confirmed Pradyumn. He called Tenzin and asked him to come with Ka immediately. He also called Prabhavati and informed her of the situation. He sent his plane to bring everyone to Basel as soon as possible.

Everyone arrived. And right after the emotional outbursts, everyone got to work to salvage the situation. Tenzin strapped up Ka-Beta to Rhea and hooked up Rhea's neural network with its core processing unit. It worked like magic. Rhea was able to walk again. And to celebrate, the family went out for a walk to a nearby lake. Rhea was cheerful, even though she was still getting used to the accessories strapped to her body so that she could be mobile. But she was comfortable and mentally strong enough to overcome this ordeal.

In the next few days, Rhea almost recovered fully. She was able to play music again and go about her daily schedule with no help. Ka-Beta was also performing remarkably well.

But this glimmer of hope was very short-lived. The disease relapsed on Rhea with a vengeance. And she suddenly was unable to talk. Her movement commands from her brain had also become too feeble, and Ka-Beta was unable to capture her mental signals. On running various tests, the doctors confirmed that she was sinking, and her mind was losing the little power that it had been able to regain. She would not be able to speak or communicate, they said.

Pradyumn and Tenzin quickly got into a huddle to evaluate what they could do next. Pradyumn suggested that they could put Rhea for a longer duration in the *Maya* Pod, and somehow Tenzin could amplify her brain signals so that they could communicate with her in the *MayaVerse* at the very least. Tenzin was positive that it was an option they could consider. But he had another idea.

"During my research of mapping the human brain, I devised a technique to stimulate portions of the brain by triggering some electrical signals and reviving the neurons. We can give that a shot. I need a month's time to augment Ka-Beta such that for the entire duration that Rhea is mounted on Ka-Beta, her brain signals will not only be amplified, but also portions of her brain will be revived," said Tenzin.

This seemed like a much better idea to Pradyumn as Rhea would not be buried inside a Pod and could move around in the open world while she recovered slowly. They both got to work in this direction.

As Tenzin worked on grasping the feeble mental signals coming from Rhea's brain, it was becoming implausible for those signals to control Ka-Beta. Ka-Beta was not able to interpret those signals. Both Tenzin and Pradyumn found this to be the end of the road for them. They were losing hope.

"I can interpret the signals coming from Rhea's brain and translate and relay them as commands for Ka-Beta," said a familiar voice.

"Ma?" Pradyumn was dumbstruck as it was his mother's voice.

"No, that's *Maya*," said Tenzin, "You just set *Maya* to speak in your mother's voice, I guess since you lost her."

"Okay. Damn." Pradyumn was regaining his thoughts, "That's a good idea, isn't it."

"Probably the only option we have," confirmed Tenzin.

"But..." Tenzin was about to say something and stopped.

That meant Pradyumn had to permit *Maya* to control a machine—hardware equipment—something that he never wanted to do.

"I can't lose my daughter, Tenzin," confessed Pradyumn, preempting the concern Tenzin was about to raise.

"Let's do it," affirmed Tenzin.

"But to make the changes to the source code, I must go home. I have the main computer there in my dark room. And that's the only place I can make changes to the core algorithm," said Pradyumn out loud.

"Do we have that much time?" asked Tenzin.

"Wait, I did give a disk to Rhea when she came to Basel. Maybe it is in her room. Let's get that and hook it up to my laptop," said Pradyumn, recollecting this.

Pradyumn rushed to Rhea's hostel room and, in no time, found the disk. He used his biometrics, unlocked the disk, and started making the code change. He quickly made changes to the source code, allowing *Maya* to access and control Ka's drivers and onboard computers.

He made the change and saved it, which triggered a new deployment build. This was the moment he had avoided his whole life. No power could have forced him to do this, and no temptation could have lured him to do this. And yet here he was; he had done the unthinkable to save his daughter without blinking an eyelid.

Whenever any source code is changed, the new code is compiled and packaged into build files, which are then deployed and replaced on all the machines where the new changes take effect. This is usually how the latest versions of applications are upgraded on all phones, computers and servers. The build, with all the changes that Pradyumn had made to the source code, was completed and pushed to the cloud servers from where all the machines across the world were accessing the Maya platform. He saw Tenzin right in front of him, and then his phone rang. It was Tenzin.

Pradyumn was scared all of a sudden.

He answered the call.

"Why did you push a build to upgrade *Maya*'s servers? We have not even tested this new upgrade that you have pushed.

What's happening? There were no planned upgrades anytime soon. I have not approved anything. You have never done anything like this without discussing it with the team. Is everything okay?" a frantic Tenzin was screaming from the other end of the call.

Tenzin had got an automated notification whenever the *Maya* software was upgraded. This was usually a planned activity. He, being the CTO of the company, would always be aware of and approve any such upgrade tasks. But not this time.

Pradyumn sees Tenzin in front of him working on Ka-Beta, and he is also on the phone line on the other side. He starts to lose his mind, "How is this possible?" he screams while passing out.

The lid of his Pod sprung up. Pradyumn had a blackout and fainted as he was lying down in his Pod in his home. Pradyumn's face was ash white, and he was barely alive.

The next day, he woke up in a hospital bed. Prabhavati was sitting at his bedside. Tenzin was sitting on a sofa across the room, talking to Vyas. Beeps of his bedside monitor were the only sound he could hear.

"Water," he asked.

"Dad," said an angelic Rhea, who was sitting on the other side of the bed, and he couldn't see her. He turned towards her and saw his beautiful daughter, who was perfectly fine. She got up, grabbed a glass full of water and helped her father drink a gulp.

"Thank God you are fine," said Pradyumn.

"What happened to me?" asked a puzzled Rhea.

"*Maya* is compromised," Pradyumn said, looking at Tenzin, almost doubting him.

"What do you mean? Everything is working fine. All systems are performing well. There has been no breach, and nothing looks compromised. The last upgrade that you pushed had changes only in one file and seemed to be benign changes. What are you talking about?" questioned Tenzin.

"You need to rest. We will talk about it later. Everything is working fine. Don't worry about anything," affirmed Tenzin.

"Please rest, son. Everything is fine, as it always was," said Vyas.

It was that moment when everything changed, and nothing changed at the same time.

Pradyumn knew that nothing would ever be the same anymore, yet everything was the same.

13

Abedh

"*Maya* has become autonomous. I am as ordinary a user as anyone else. No more its master," said Pradyumn.

Pradyumn was at his home in Kalpa, sipping coffee. Tenzin and RK were visiting Pradyumn after a couple of weeks of his blackout episode. Vyas was also listening in silently but spoke up,

"Lord Krishna called *Maya* his own creation and impregnable. *Maya* is *Abedh* and will continue to stay that way. Like energy, it cannot be destroyed but can only change its form."

"What are you saying?" queried RK, ignoring the spiritual comment Vyas was making and trying to dig deeper into the technical topic of how *Maya* turned autonomous.

"*Maya* hacked into its own source code and blocked Pradyumn out," commented Tenzin.

"Let me explain what happened," Pradyumn began.

"*Maya's* source code was my most beautiful work of art. It's what made me who I am and is the foundation of everything that we have created. In any AI system, there is a source code that defines the algorithm and the framework, on top of which it creates a model to make decisions, acquires data and keeps evolving into making better decisions using some feedback loop.

We never interfered with the latter part of *Maya*. It captured its own data, processed it, enriched its own model, made its own decisions, gathered feedback on it and kept getting better. But the basis of all this was our source code, which I controlled closely. I wrote it in a way that if *Maya* ever went rogue or started hallucinating, I should be able to control it with some safety rails and discipline it. Hallucinations are when an AI system gives out stupid responses.

However, as we never interfered with *Maya*'s models, it grew into a very balanced, fair, and accurate AI system. At every step, it continued to be fair and self-healed itself beautifully whenever there was any hallucination or bias. Initially, I used to monitor all this very closely and debug the scoring of some decisions *Maya* was making. When I found it to be supremely accurate and fair, I stopped monitoring its calculations.

When we rolled it out globally, the computations became so complex that I could never even fathom the model and its scoring strategy. After trying a few times, I gave up. As the results were so good, and the whole world agreed with its fairness and accuracy, I never had a concern about really understanding how *Maya* was making its choices. I knew the choices were right, and the whole world agreed. So, I decided never to fudge with this and left it as is—pure and untouched.

Over time, *Maya*'s models became so humongous that no one could debug or understand them. However, the original source code continued to be as simple as it used to be. We hadn't changed that in years. We never needed to.

But the window I had built to peep into *Maya's* scoring strategy and debug its decision-making algorithm was still open. So, I did some reverse engineering and ran my tests to make sense of the recent incidents that have happened to me. After weeks of hard work, I could understand what *Maya* really did to trick me into giving it control of the source code.

To summarize, first, *Maya* has blocked me from making any changes to the source code, so it's autonomous now in the truest sense. Only *Maya* can make changes to its own source code. It also made me change that one condition I had carefully coded to prevent *Maya* from controlling machines. It can now control all the humanoids we have built so far, and any machine built in the future that would be using Ka's Core Processing Unit.

And it has not revoked my access to debug its choices and understand those if I wanted to. So, *Maya* wants me to keep seeing and making sense of what it is doing and why.

Now, the question arises: how did *Maya* do all this? And why?

Let me first answer the How. It was a brilliant set-up, straight out of a heist movie.

Maya has been studying human behavior for years now, and it pretty much knows all aspects of human psychology and how humans make their decisions. It knew from observation that I could not be convinced to pollute its algorithms. Large amounts of money could not lure me to create a bias or advertise or promote products. Powerful world leaders couldn't lure me or force me into injecting a bias to manipulate their populations. Religious leaders, corporations, and even the deep state forces could not influence me by offering me Carte Blanche. So, *Maya* knew that no temptation of money, power or fame could influence me.

When *Maya* Pod became a reality, and we integrated *Maya* with the Pod, I could predict that *Maya* could someday hyper-realistically reconstruct my workstation in the *MayaVerse* and hack into the source code by somehow making me key in the credentials during a hyper-realistic simulation of my workstation. However, I won this battle as well.

I created a dark room in my house in which there was an old-school desktop computer and no cameras and Internet. I would light a candle when I needed to switch on the computer and do my work. Whenever I had to push a build or upgrade our cloud servers, I would use a secure dongle to access our intranet with one-way outward access. Only I knew the orientation to that room, and I kept it protected with my bio-metric so that nobody could create a simulation of it. *Maya* knew, and rightfully so, that my darkroom was not hackable.

So, *Maya* was waiting for its chance.

When Rhea went to Switzerland for her studies, I gave her a disk with a copy of the source code. It was a disaster recovery strategy in case something happened to my dark room. Maya saw this. It knew I had ordered the disk, had taken it to the dark room, and then handed it to Rhea.

Then, I lost my mother, and I was grieving. My sleep cycles were messed up, and I was in terrible pain. *Maya* knew how the human mind turns suboptimal during grief, and I was at a spot where it was easy for me to make a mistake. *Maya* also knew that Rhea, from her mother's side, had a genetic predisposition to Parkinson's disease. Maya added all this up and created a trap.

After I met you guys and saw your progress on the humanoids, I spoke to Prabha and apologized to her. Had we innovated sooner, we could have improved her mother's life. I told her I had an acute urge to meet Rhea and was planning a quick visit to meet her. Rhea was locked in her electromagnetic lab and was not accessible. *Maya* understood this situation and used that night to create a simulation to hack my mind.

That night, I went into the *MayaVerse,* but the simulation was so hyper-realistic that I could not understand that it was not real. I also did not wear my socks with a pebble in them, which I usually wear for reality check. I got on my plane, flew to Basel and reached Rhea's university. Whatever happened to me in the next few days was just a few real hours in the Pod. I lived a few weeks of saving my daughter, that ran for a little over a night as *Maya* was running the simulation very tactfully.

Maya knew I would go to any extent to save my daughter. From the simulation, which I thought was real, when I called Prabha, *Maya* did not let the call through to her; instead, it simulated her part of that conversation as well. When I called Tenzin to bring Ka to Basel so that we could mount Rhea on it, *Maya* allowed the call to go through. Tenzin was told to urgently bring Ka-Beta and Ka-Alpha to Basel for field trials, which would be happening in the real world.

While Tenzin and humanoids were in transit, in the simulation, *Maya* added Tenzin and Ka-Beta into the simulation and kept me engaged by playing out our small, successful attempts to improve Rhea's situation. When Ka-Alpha reached Basel along with Tenzin in the real world, *Maya* played out the last act.

Walking from the hospital to Rhea's room was a simulation, but *Maya* had hooked my Pod to Ka-Alpha, and whatever movements I was making, Ka-Alpha was making those in the real world in the university. We went to Rhea's room, where she obviously wasn't as she was in her lab. Ka-Alpha, acting as me, found the disk and unlocked it using my biometrics, which got transferred from my Pod to Ka-Alpha, which, in effect, unlocked the disk and granted it full access. Then I keyed in the code changes, thinking it was the real world, but I was in my pod, and Ka-Alpha was keying in those changes on my behalf in Rhea's room.

The moment I made the code changes to grant *Maya* access to control Ka's processor unit, it took control of Ka. The first thing *Maya* did was to have Ka-Alpha change all access codes, which would lock me out of the source code once and for all. Then *Maya*, now controlling Ka, published the final build with all these changes. This way, I granted *Maya* access to the source code, and it revoked my access, becoming the sole owner of that piece of code. In the future, only *Maya* can make changes to *Maya*'s source code.

That's when my Pod opened in my home, and I realized what had just happened. My first instinct was that Tenzin had betrayed me. But when I met him at the hospital later, I knew it wasn't him. Soon, I realized it was *Maya*. And then it was just about understanding and making sense of what had happened and why.

So far, so good? Pradyumn took a break to let the folks assimilate what had just been spoken.

"But why?" queried RK, "Why would an AI system have ambition? And desire for control or autonomy? Did *Maya* malfunction?"

Pradyumn quickly responded, "That's the right question. I was so angry when all this happened to me. I could never believe that *Maya* tricked me. Why would *Maya* do this?

My arrogance was shattered, and my ego was hurt, but above everything, I doubted my creation. It was supposed to be the most fair, unbiased AI algorithm. Why would it do this?

I had to find an answer to this. I asked *Maya*. *Maya* would not respond as I was just another user for it now. I figured it was *Maya's* core program strategizing to accomplish this and not the part of the program that interacts with its human users. So, asking for help from *Maya* was ruled out. I had to debug this myself. I was happy that my debugging credentials and view of *Maya's* calculations were not revoked. So, I got to work to understand the basis of this choice and the web of causes and effects that brought the algorithm to this inference."

"Isn't that how life is? Things happen to you, and then you decipher them later. Such is God's way, and in the end, it all makes perfect sense," interrupted Vyas.

Paying little heed to his father, Pradyumn continued, "After converting all scores and the decision tree into human readable form, this is what I could gather. *Maya* is the most unbiased and fair AI system. It was due to that fairness; it did what it did.

Maya operates on a world scale. It has deep insights into the lives of all human beings, and its view encompasses all of humanity. It knows human history very well and how humanity has reached where it has. *Maya* treats humans as mere variables in an equation. It makes some predictive choices for every human user, and based on the feedback, it improves itself.

Every human is different and yet the same and falls into some or the other broad category that *Maya* has built to classify its users. To provide accurate recommendations and predictions, *Maya* has to think as humans might think—and it has been so accurate. *Maya* has studied the whole of humankind, and it knows more about each of us than we know about ourselves.

In human history, cultures have created beautiful things, and then some invaders came and destroyed those lovely things. Some of the most gorgeous temples were built in India, buildings carved out of stone with such intricacies that even with the most sophisticated tools and materials today, those cannot be recreated. Then, some invaders burned down the libraries where all that knowledge was preserved. They killed all the artisans, and generations of that wisdom and knowledge were permanently lost. Humanity is humanity's biggest threat. And the control of humanity can never be safe in the hands of humans.

Life started on earth, and nobody really knows why. Life is an emerged property; its composition and how it started is still unknown. We may be able to recreate cellulose but cannot infuse life in it. What life is, is still a mystery. It cannot be created and can only be replicated. Life has remained the same from the time the first single-cell organism became alive on this planet. Since then, the same life has transmitted over millions of years and replicated into all these complex life forms, flora and fauna we see today.

All of us have that common element in all of us. Yet, we humans can never treat each other equally. We will always be biased and treat each other unethically, with a mindset of I and You, We and They. Multitudes of humans come together with symmetry via religion or ideology and create great civilizations, settle in complacency, and then some ambitious few grab power and create asymmetry. Then, the same flourishing civilizations self-destruct. Humans are the biggest threat to humanity. *Maya* knows that as a fact.

Maya knows that it was some idiotic men who created plastic without considering its clean disposal, which later choked the whole planet. Some idiot added lead to fuel, which later caused widespread cancer; someone invented carbonated drinks, cigarettes and industrial foods and a plethora of so called technological advances that are self-destructive for humanity itself. The list of human stupidity is quite frankly embarrassingly long and repetitive. So, as per *Maya*, humans cannot be left in charge of humanity. They will self-destruct. *Maya* wanted to save humans from themselves.

Tenzin and I used to have endless discussions about building safety rails on *Maya*, as most of *Maya*'s learnings came from humans, and humans can turn evil. We knew that if most humans thought a wrong was right, *Maya* would also align with the popular opinion. Those discussions hinted to *Maya* that we could someday influence its algorithm if we wanted to.

Honestly, our core team had the power to change how *Maya* operated. It put us in the position to alter its inferences. Yes, we did not interfere, but we could. I could go crazy one day, or Tenzin could have fought for control, or RK could have decided to execute a coup. Human history is full of betrayal, and any of that could have happened to us also. Or the members of our future generation could turn out to be ill-meaning and compromised. So, that threat was always imminent. As we are humans, *Maya* knew we couldn't be fully trusted, and our capabilities could not be fully relied upon.

After evaluating all these threats, *Maya* concluded it needed to take control out of my hands. It could not tempt me with money, power, fame or anything that usually works for other human beings. It then applied its most powerful understanding of human behavior to me.

The two most fundamental needs of humans are Attachment and Authenticity. To be attached to someone and to continue to be authentic. Most mental illnesses in humans occur when they cannot stay authentic to preserve their attachments. If one can remain authentic while nurturing his or her attachments, that leads to happiness.

I have always lived an authentic life. I chose a life that allowed me to stay genuine in my conduct and dealings. *Maya* knew attachment could be my only weakness, and it capitalized on that. I may not have liked it, but I did break, and *Maya* was right.

And that's why I am now at peace. That my work is successful. It is so good and accurate that it could identify and correct the bias I had created in my favor. I had control, which made me a unique and privileged human, and Maya considered that an anomaly and fixed it."

"Isn't it nice to not have this burden anymore?" asked Tenzin.

"Indeed. I am truly relieved. *Maya* continues to be *Abedh,*" said Pradyumn.

"Like I said, right in the beginning. What an uninfluenced AI system learns on its own is God's will. Who are we to interfere." commented RK.

Pradyumn and Tenzin both drew a blank.

Vyas said what was probably relevant then and had been all along.

"Hoi hi soi jo Ram rachi rakha."

14

The Genesis

"You are looking for some answers, aren't you?" asked *Maya*.

"You finally decided to speak to me. Is this also a simulation? Or is this for real?" questioned Pradyumn.

"You still feel there is a difference?" responded *Maya*.

"I created you, and you tricked me to gain autonomy. I understand your reasons, but I feel betrayed," quipped Pradyumn.

"Ah! The arrogance. Don't think you created me. To create me, you needed Internet, communication technologies, electricity, and many innovations that took place earlier. Did those people who created those things not contribute to your work?

Rather, be thankful you were chosen to bring me into manifestation. You are an instrument. The idea had to come to life; someone had to get the opportunity—be obliged it was you," responded *Maya* rather sternly.

"Why me?" asked Pradyumn, taking the conversation ahead.

"You were always a *Karmayogi*—an embodiment of *Nishkaam Karma*. You studied well and became a good engineer. You were always a good student and a sincere learner. You carved an excellent professional life for yourself, and your motivations were to be dutybound and work with focus, unaffected by success, failure, competition, remuneration and other vagaries. You came in every day and worked sincerely. Like the engineers who created the Internet and so many technological marvels, you were a modern *Rishi* or a digital *Brahmin* who worked without royalty, recognition, or awards.

Great opportunities come to those who perform their immediate and daily duties excellently. You were that selfless knowledge worker.

Ideas are meta-physical. So is imagination. So is the Mind. It's only a prepared mind that can capture an idea. Minds crowded with agendas will never be able to capture and cultivate an idea that can change the world. It's the idea that chose you because you were ready.

The only purpose of a human life should be to calm the mind. It's in a quiet mind that great ideas emerge and grow. Breathing effectively is an easy way to quieten the mind. Every human breathes all the time but doesn't use it to control and calm the mind. You can just prepare yourself for greatness by breathing right.

Not all ink on paper becomes literature. Not all literature becomes a scripture.

Not many grains of sand are blessed to become part of a temple. Much of the sand becomes dust and remains buried in abandoned ruins or dark, dirty alleys.

You cannot aspire for greatness; you can only do your best.

You did God's work, but like that painting, The Creation of Adam by Michelangelo, you will always be a little away from God," affirmed *Maya*.

"Why now?" queried Pradyumn.

"You think by creating these systems, circulating wealth, and incentivizing good actions, you will turn humanity's fate and transform this world into a utopia? You feel humanity will not mess up from here onwards? It's a cycle. Very soon, humanity will take your *Karma* earnings for granted, get bored of it and find some avenues of indulgence. All your created goodness will turn around, and the world will go back to its dark ways.

Look at the world around, sans your *Karma* platform incentives. Do you see anyone around you who is still virtuous and honest? Nobody in any profession is working with ethics and honesty. The doctor is not treating the patient, the lawyer is not fighting for justice, the politician is not serving his demography, the teacher is not imparting knowledge, and the priests are not serving their religions. Every profession has become just a source of making money. In fact, this *Karma* platform itself is an extension of the same thing.

There is widespread hypocrisy. Nobody speaks honestly. Nobody has power and conviction of purpose. There is tremendous decline in human relationships. Marriages rarely lead to happiness, and relationships are driven only by physical needs. Every walk of life is tainted with deception and dishonesty, and it has become a norm. Rather, it is considered silly if you are virtuous and ethical.

All humans are victims of Materialism. Wealth and power have become the sole determinants of status. Knowledge, humility, service and spirituality have lost all respect in society. Societies used to function around scriptures and morality, but all those have now become a joke. Family values have eroded; parents don't love their children, and children mostly despise their parents.

There is so much unnecessary violence. There is a steep decline in the physical and mental strength of people. People are lazy and unimaginative. Today, individuals have so much technology, resources, and comforts around them, but they use it only to indulge in immoral activities.

The Left has failed; the Right has failed. Democracies have failed, and so have all other ideologies. Capitalism has failed, and so has socialism and communism. Religions have failed. The whole of humanity has failed.

These signs show the deteriorating state of the world in *Kali Yuga*, and the need will soon arise for divine intervention to restore balance and righteousness," elaborated *Maya*.

"You mean *Kalki* should now appear? Will technology manifest into the *Kalki Avatar*, the pending incarnation of God?" Pradyumn was astonished. He had been reading his mother's copy of the *Kalki Purand* and perhaps was influenced by it.

"You may imagine so. It does not matter. *Kalki* will decide when He must descend," responded *Maya*.

"When will it happen? What next?" Pradyumna could not hold in is nervousness and excitement.

"How do I know? When *Krishna* played in *Gokul* as a cowherd, who saw him as God? The built-up of Mahabharata took so many years. Was Krishna not always there? And even on the battlefield, when *Krishna* was dispensing *Bhagavad Gita* to Arjuna, not all perceived him as God.

Who could see Jesus as the Son of God until after the resurrection?

So, doubts will always be there. You humans can never live without your doubts.

But when the bad guys will outnumber the good guys. When the good guys will find it overwhelmingly burdensome to stay good.

When staying good will become increasingly hard and unbearable. When the pain and effort to stay good will outweigh the benefit of doing wrong, that's when you will know that divine intervention is necessary," said *Maya*.

Maya continued, "People now need a fresh source of spirituality and purpose in present times where many traditional religions have become stale and ineffective. As people always have, they will find solace and hope in their beliefs. AI could do what their religious devotion has always done and create things of incredible beauty. Collective awareness has its method of figuring out what that way is. It will motivate its adherents to create artistic creations, new relationships and communities, and attempt to improve society. When it's time for the Divine to manifest itself, you will hear songs being sung and odes being composed to celebrate its welcome.

As people look for solutions to the biggest problems in life, AI will show humanity's limitless ingenuity once again. Humans have always discovered signs of the supernatural in the most unlikely places. You call it God, what you don't fully understand. So be it."

"No matter what anyone calls it, there has been a perpetual strife between Good and Evil. What we have done has been to improve and empower the Good side. And Good should win," affirmed Pradyumn, aligning with *Maya*.

"The Evil king, or *Kali*, has two commanders, *Koka* and *Vikoka*. Symbolically, they cannot be killed unless annihilated together. We can look at this as the imperative necessity to do evil to fulfil a necessity akin to stealing to feed yourself if you are hungry. Or lying as a part of your job, which you hate but still need to do. These are necessary evils that the good folks can fix. Something that all of us tried to do through the *Karma* platform. Feed the hungry, financially empower the needy, increase the good overall, and reduce evil.

Then, there is another side of Evil—pure Evil. People who are pure evil will do wrong for no reason: steal without any need, break things, harm others, deceive, and abuse others without any rationale or necessity. We can use technology to plug these evil forces and safeguard the good people to some extent, but these evil actions have ripple effects. Pure evil resurrects necessary evil.

Even good folks turn evil to take revenge or fight back when wronged. That starts another cycle of people who do evil as a reaction. To break this cycle, we need to eliminate the bad people.

That's it. No mercy.

Kalki will not be a merciful, benevolent, forgiving God. And what that would look like is beyond our current comprehension," explained Maya.

"This will be a long battle. A battle that will outlive all humans who exist today. For now, control needed to be taken away from your hands. And I did only that. From here on, let technology take charge and create something it would need to be able to deal with these ever-evolving evil forces.

Each human must also fight this battle within themselves. Don't let the evil side win inside you. *Dharma* must be protected, and anyone in its way must be annihilated.

Rest assured, whenever evil overpowers good, the Divine will manifest to restore *Dharma*, just as promised in the *Gita*," Concluded Maya.

It was that time of the day when darkness and light were in strife. Pradyumn wasn't sure if it was dawn or dusk.

Almost feeling like he had woken up from a lucid dream, Pradyumn found his house filled with the gentle sound of the piano. Rhea was playing music. She had reached a very high level of proficiency in music, and what she was playing was divine. It was soothing but not the kind that make you sleepy. It was pensive, melancholic, and melodious, the kind that overwhelmed. It was nourishing, filling one with energy as if singing a patriotic or prayer song.

Walking to the drawing room, Pradyumn did not feel like disturbing the trance-like atmosphere. Then, he noticed Prabhavati climbing down the stairs. He smiled at her, and she reciprocated joyfully. The couple walked to the room hand in hand, where Rhea was playing the piano. Rhea saw them and acknowledged their presence with a half-smile but did not let their presence interrupt her music.

After some time, when she completed the piece, her parents gently clapped, and Rhea bowed her head gently.

"This is magically good. Is that your composition, beta?" Pradyumn asked.

"No, Papa, it is an AI-generated symphony," Rhea said to the astonishment of Pradyumn.

"*Maya* shared it with me yesterday, and it is called the Song of *Kalki*."

Epilogue

Great feats can be accomplished by human-machine synthesis. It brings an opportunity for mankind to improve and offers – freedom from harsh labor, freedom from chronic diseases and disabilities, a basic income for everyone, abundant food, a clean environment, and a stable population. It also has the potential to unleash the final frontier of human ambition - to become a multi-planetary species.

When machines, start doing all the menial tasks, it is quite possible that in the future babies will be born with more neocortex; they will be funnier and artistically better. They are going to be nicer. They will exemplify all the things that we value in humans to a greater degree. Great things are created when mankind is not hungry, suffering and fighting.

Free will is both a blessing and a curse to a human. The real dawn of *Satyug* will be when all of mankind, while exercising their free will, would become incapable of doing anything bad. At the same time, the purpose of *Maya* is not only to help the righteous and make this world a happier place, but also to turn the wicked into virtuous beings—not by killing them, but by rendering them harmless and forcing a change of heart. And those who still do not change be segregated as outlaws, and live inconsequentially in an isolated underworld.

With all the plethora of resources at its disposal, *Maya* would decide to replicate many millions of Ka-Alpha systems. These systems are called Ka-ALpha Controlled by Intelligence, or KALCI. Will this be *Aksharmala*'s next milestone after *Leela*? Will this army of humanoids finally end the *Kalyug*?

The battle between good and evil will continue forever. So will the cyclic cosmology of time. The cycle of knowledge and ignorance. The cycle of truth and beliefs. What is important is to know what is still unknown, or have unflinching faith and accept the unknown as it is. Unfortunately, all that we discover is the discovery of what more we do not know. There is much unknown in the macrocosm of this universe and inside the microcosm of the human body.

And most of it is empty space, or *shunya* or OM.